SAVING
WONDER

SAVING WONDER

WONDER

MARY KNIGHT

SCHOLASTIC INC.

ISBN 978-1-338-60333-0

10 9 8 7 6 5 4 3 2 1   19 20 21 22 23

Printed in the U.S.A.   40
This edition first printing, 2019

Book design by Ellen Duda

Dictionary definitions at the end of chapters C, D, E, F, I, K, L (first entry),
P, Q, V, W, X, and Y were taken from *Webster's Revised Unabridged Dictionary*
(1913 edition); the definition at the end of chapter U was taken from *An
American Dictionary of the English Language* (1828 edition). All other
definitions were written by the author.

In loving memory of
Other Daddy, who gave his daughters a love for words,
and
Mom, who passed it on

Wisdom begins in wonder.

—Socrates

Ever since I can remember, Papaw's been giving me words. Every week a new word, beginning with *a* and running through the alphabet twice a year. It's a perfect system, or so Papaw says. "It's as if the calendar folks and the alphabet folks planned it that way." He gives me the word on a Sunday and I'm supposed to use it every day of the week. Some words I take a shine to more than others. *Lackadaisical* is one of my favorites. I like the way it rolls off my tongue.

The kids at school up in Fraleysburg aren't too keen on my words, so Papaw and I mostly use them at home here in Wonder Gap. Sometimes when I let one slip, they make fun of me. Now that I'm in seventh grade, it's even worse. Like when Carl Jenkins dropped his lunch tray next to me and his fruit cocktail shot out in every direction all mixed up with his spaghetti and meatballs. When I looked down and saw what had happened, I blurted out: "Gee, Carl, that's a verifiable mess you got there." Well, he was on me like a coyote in a barnyard of chickens.

I think it was that black eye that caused Papaw to *acquiesce* (first word, this year). "No use using 'em where they ain't working," he said, agreeing to keep my words to ourselves.

"So what's the use of using them at all?" I said, holding a pack of frozen peas over my right eye and feeling downright *belligerent* (second word, this year).

"Well, Curley, words are your way out of the holler," he said.

Papaw always says that, even though he's never asked me if I wanted to go. I love my papaw, so it's hard to argue with him. Besides, he's all I've got.

My daddy died in a coal mining accident right after my little brother, Zeb, was born. I hardly remember him. Four years later, Ma and Zeb were gone, too, swallowed up by a river of sludge. It had been raining hard all week, and the coal company's slurry pond at the top of the mountain over from ours broke through its walls. A thick stream of black mud came cascading down the holler, covering everything in its path. Ma and little Zeb were winding their way back home from old Ida's house along the creek bed. I guess they couldn't get out of the way fast enough.

Papaw came to get me at school that afternoon. "Your ma and little Zeb are gone" was all he said. "Just you and me now, Curley. We're all we've got." Papaw was Ma's pa. He'd been staying with us since my daddy died, Papaw being a widower and all.

For the rest of the day after Papaw told me, I simmered in a world of hurt, wondering how Ma could have up and left me like that—taking Zeb with her and not me. It wasn't until we showed up at the Donnelly house for the viewing that I realized they weren't just gone, but dead. I know that sounds weird, but Papaw says our minds try to protect us from a painful truth for as long as they can. Papaw also says I kicked his shins black and blue that day, but that he deserved it for not finding a better way to tell me that terrible news.

My mother and brother were found on the banks of Miller Creek. I've often wondered what caught Sheriff Whitaker's eye. Was it the pale hand of my mother reaching high out of the muck like she knew the answer? I'm told she was clinging tight to little Zeb in her other arm.

Ida Donnelly and her sister, Rosa May, took over cleaning up the bodies. They washed them in an old claw-foot tub in their backyard. Papaw said he'd forever be obliged to them for that. He didn't think he could have done it himself and gone on living.

They put Ma and little Zeb in a coffin together, wrapped in a quilt, and buried them up on a grassy plateau by my daddy's grave with a view of our holler. Lots of folks came to the funeral. The Donnelly sisters were there, of course, and my friend, Jules, and her ma, Irene. A whole slew of miners stood back a ways, clumped together like coal, their faces all shadowy gray. They must have come right from the night shift that let out that morning, but the day shift was glaringly absent. That was back when I was seven, and things still haven't changed. Far as I can tell, here in eastern Kentucky, nothing ever does. The mines don't stop working for nobody, Papaw says, not even for one of their own.

Mr. Barkley, the owner of the mine, didn't even have the decency to show up for Mama and little Zeb's funeral. Papaw said it had something to do with not wanting to show culpability, which at the time was a word I didn't understand. The manager of the mine was standing with the others, though—Antoine Martin, a fancy name that no one had the patience for, so they called him Antsy for short. Folks say he's always fidgeting about something, but that day he was standing stock-still. All through "Amazing Grace," I gave him my evil eye.

Preacher Jones handed me the shovel after he said a few words. I guess he wanted me to throw down some dirt, but I threw the shovel instead. It clunked and clattered against the wooden casket as a hush settled on everyone there. No word seemed big enough for the mad I felt. Later, Papaw told me I said, "This whole thing is absolutely futile," before I broke from his arms and ran all the way home.

Futile. That was the word for the week, as you might have guessed. Papaw and I couldn't bring ourselves to use it again after that, but the word sat between us nonetheless.

I guess I should tell you something about myself. My name's Curley Hines. Well, actually, it's Michael Weaver Hines, but my folks started calling me Curly on account of my hair. I added the *e* in grade school so it wouldn't look so girly. I think it helps.

Anyway, Michael and Hines I get from my daddy. Weaver's from Mama's side and Papaw's last name. Both sides of my people are Scotch-Irish, come over from the old world to settle in the new. The way Papaw tells it, they pushed west until they recognized the green of the hills and called Appalachia home.

I may as well tell you I have a girlfriend. She lives down the holler from me and her name's Julia Cavanaugh, or Jules for short. I told her once that her name reminds me of treasure, and she kind of liked the idea. Our mothers were friends when we were babies. They'd pack us up on hot summer days and take us to play in the creek or pick wild-flowers up on Red Hawk Mountain. We like to say we've got history, which, of course, is true. I know her better than any-body besides my family. Come to think of it, I guess I know her more.

My birthday's this Tuesday, so Papaw said I could invite any friend I wanted over for Sunday dinner to celebrate. He said it that way on the off chance I might invite somebody other than Jules, not that he has anything against her. He's just always saying I need to "widen my circle," which means he doesn't want me to get too attached to anything—friends or mountains—that will keep me from eventually leav-ing home.

I know he means well, but I think I'm a lost cause. I've been attached to these mountains since I was born, like my umbilical cord was lassoed around their tops. I know that sounds extreme and maybe even gross, but that's how it feels. And then, after Ma and little Zeb died, the mountains were the only thing that kept me from flying apart—them and Papaw, of course. Jules understands this. She loves the mountains, too.

Papaw sighed when I told him I'd invited Jules, but then he said, "Well, *good*."

In that my birthday is January 21, it often falls on a *c* word. Papaw spends extra time flipping through the dictionary the week before, looking for just the right one. During last year's birthday week, my word was *collaborate*, the kind of word that Papaw hopes will stick with me and guide my ways. Papaw's always reminding me that words are more than a mishmash of letters and sounds.

"Words are thoughts and thoughts are things," he says, which makes no sense to me, but he promises I'll grow into the idea.

Papaw seems particularly pleased with his pick for this year's birthday word. He's been chuckling about it all week. I've been yammering for a hint all day, but he says he wants to wait for Jules to get here before he gives me my first clue.

Jules makes an entrance, as usual. I mean, she doesn't mean to. She doesn't even know she does. It's just that when she's not there, something always seems missing, and when she's there, the room seems all of a sudden full.

That's how it is when she bursts through the front door, all red-cheeked and breathy, her frizzy black hair bushing out from under a blue knit cap.

"Brought you something," she says, slapping a square-looking package against her jeans to shake off the snow before handing it to me. "You can open it after dinner, I guess."

The package is wrapped in burlap and tied with a scrap of yellow silk ribbon, probably from her ma's sewing basket. Jules and her ma go up to the Kmart in Fraleysburg on a regular basis, so it's not as if wrapping paper isn't available. As Papaw explains it, Mrs. Cavanaugh was raised by a couple of back-to-earth hippies and prefers to make do with what she's got.

"Hey, Mr. Weaver, what's cookin'?" Jules calls to Papaw, throwing her coat on a rack by the door and brushing by me on her way to the kitchen.

"Gee, thanks, Jules," I say, looking down at my present.

You'll never catch Jules being sentimental about anything, incidentally. Not birthdays. Not holidays. Not puppies or kittens. Not love. Especially not love.

That didn't used to be a problem.

I know I said she was my girlfriend, and she is. I've even heard her call me her boyfriend to her friends at school. But—

8

and this is a big "but"—she always adds, "Just not in *that way*." Like I said, that didn't used to be a problem.

"I'm thinking of a word and it begins with *c*," Papaw says, beginning the word game we play every Sunday. He gives Jules the silverware and me the plates to set the table. "This one's a little different from your usual birthday word, Curley. Now that you're entering your man years, you need to find a way to *articulate*"—(first word, last year)—"what a *puzzle* this world can be." Papaw always pauses at the clues when it's time to guess, so I can tell *puzzle* is one of them. So does Jules.

"Hmmm, I think this one's a stumper," she says, carefully setting the forks to the left and the knives to the right of the plates. "What do you think, birthday boy?"

"It's right on the tip of my tongue," I lie as I look at her across the table. All I can think about is the way her tawny skin dimples when she smiles, creating a tiny cave in only one of her cheeks. I've wanted to stick my finger into that dimple for as long as I can remember, but I figure she'd kill me if I ever tried.

"Well, I'm sure there's no *problem* the two of you can't figure out when you put your heads together," Papaw says, chuckling, "even if it seems *unsolvable*."

Jules plops herself down in Ma's rocker by the cookstove, drawing her knees up under the oversized flannel shirt she's wearing. She gets those rocker legs rolling tip to tip so hard they make the oak floor rumble.

"I think this was a vocabulary word in Mrs. Rosen's class last year, Curley," Jules says over the thunder she's making. "You know this one."

The word all of a sudden pops into my head, like Jules willed it there. I remember it because we spent an entire day in Mrs. Rosen's English class making up riddles and puns that made absolutely no sense at all.

"*Conundrum*? Is that it, Papaw?"

He smiles and nods.

"Aw, that was easy," I say, like I ever would have gotten it without Jules zapping it over to me on that telepathic high-way of hers.

"Easy to say, maybe, but never easy to understand." Papaw stirs the gravy. "Life's a conundrum, my friends. Some mysteries were never meant to be solved."

Just then, we hear a thump, thump, thump at the front door.

"Now, who could that be?" Papaw raps the gravy spoon twice on the side of the cast-iron skillet. "Curley, go see who it is."

I swing the door open with what must be a goofy grin on my face. Honestly, I think maybe it's a surprise visitor for my birthday, although I can't imagine who that would be. The last person I expect to see is Antsy Martin.

"Hey, Curley." He nods at me and takes off his cap. He always does that. It's like he's paying respects to the dead every time he sees me.

"Mr. Martin." I nod back. I'm not about to invite him in. Neither is Papaw when he shows up beside me.

"Antsy? What the heck?" Papaw stretches his long arm out and leans against the doorframe, like he's barring the way in. "Curley, you and Jules go put milk on the table. I'll take care of this."

As I turn to leave, I overhear Antsy saying, "Sorry, John, I know you told me never to come by when the boy might be home." He's talking in a low raspy voice, but I can hear him as clear as rain on a tin roof. It's like my ears get all supersized when I hear he's talking about me. I hide behind the coatrack to listen.

"Yeah, that's right, Martin . . . which is why this better be good." When Papaw draws his words out all slow and easy like that, you know you're in trouble. But what can Antsy possibly want on a Sunday afternoon? And what's so all-fired secret they don't want me to hear it?

"That's just it, John—it isn't good." There's a long pause while Antsy clears his throat and spits. I'm assuming he does that right outside the door, and I gag silently, thinking about it sitting there on the porch all brown and globby.

"John, the mine's getting a new owner. Barkley is selling out to some big corporation up in Indiana, and the new owner is coming down next week."

I guess this is big news for some in these parts, but for the life of me, I can't figure out why Antsy thinks Papaw would even care. It's no secret that Papaw's not exactly a friend of coal, although since Mama and Zeb died, he's kept what he calls his "spit and vinegar" to himself. You'd think it would be the opposite, but when I gave him an I ♥ MOUNTAINS bumper sticker for his van last Christmas, he used it for a bookmark—shut up all tight between the pages of his dusty old spy novels.

Speaking of spies, my eyes just about pop out of my head when I see Antsy hand Papaw a short, padded white envelope. "This may be the last one of these," Antsy says as Papaw stuffs the envelope into his front pocket.

I'm standing behind the coatrack, scratching my head

over what I've just seen, when Papaw turns around and sees me. I swear he's got eyes in the back of his head. "Go on, boy. This doesn't concern you. I gave you a job to do." He nods toward the kitchen, so I skedaddle on out of there.

I'm chewing on what might be in the envelope as I return to the kitchen and see Jules still rockin' away. Any thoughts of intrigue melt at the sight of her, sitting there all dreamlike, gazing out the window at the falling snow. She doesn't even look up at me.

I pull the milk carton from the top shelf of the fridge. It's got the face of one of those missing kids on the back of it. He's got curly hair just like me. "Hey, Jules." I put the carton up next to my face so she can see the resemblance. "Do you think I might have another family somewhere?" I'll do anything to get her attention.

But Jules, she just keeps on rocking. Obviously, she's not in the mood for goofing around, which has been happening a lot lately. Girls are a conundrum, that's for sure.

"Sooo . . . how about grabbing some glasses down from the cabinet, then?" I ask, taking a swig of milk from the carton.

Now she's staring at me with those soulful brown eyes of hers, and I wonder if she's got a crush on me, since I'm turning twelve and all—but no.

"Oh, right." I roll my eyes at her. "Pleeease?" I squeeze out the word *please* like it's a blob of crusty old toothpaste at the end of a rolled-up tube, and then I stick my tongue out at her for good measure. She slides out of the rocker, ignoring me, as usual.

Sometimes it feels like we're married.

"Anything wrong?" Jules jerks her head in the direction of the front door. She sets the glasses down in front of each plate and I pour.

"Naw, just Antsy Martin for Papaw on some kind of business. I think it's about a conundrum or something." She looks over at me and grins.

"Well now, where were we?" Papaw lumbers back into the kitchen, rubbing his hands together like he's just come back from the bathroom and not some covert operation. "Oh, that's right . . . Life's a conundrum and there's a meat loaf in the oven."

He sounds so lackadaisical about whatever just transpired with Antsy that I almost believe it isn't anything to fret about. But then I notice the top edge of that envelope sticking out of his pocket, and all I can think is *payoff*.

"Come on, you two . . . dinner's ready."

Papaw pulls my birthday meat loaf and a tray of biscuits out of the oven, and the smell just about knocks me over. My stomach starts growling like I haven't eaten in days. Whatever Papaw's conundrum is about, I'll think on it later.

After dinner, we retire to the living room, where Papaw stokes the fire in the woodstove and gets it blazing. He eases himself into his overstuffed chair. This is the time of the evening when lots of families in Wonder Gap are turning on the old "boob tube," as Papaw would call it, and watching *Celebrity Tonight* or *Gossip Hollywood* about all those movie stars, or maybe they've been watching football all day long.

Believe me, I've been campaigning for cable ever since I could talk. But Papaw says owning a TV is bowing to *mediocrity* (*m* word, last April), which basically means it turns your brain to mush. When I gave Papaw the TV-is-educational argument, he handed me an issue of *National Geographic* and said there were hundreds more like it where that came from.

"Curley, your very own Discovery Channel is waiting for you right up those attic stairs."

I haven't asked for a TV—or a computer, for that matter—since.

Jules lies across from me against the opposite arm of the couch. We throw one of Mama's quilts over us and stretch out our legs until our toes touch. I guess it's the warmth of the room and a full stomach that makes me let down my guard and start bragging.

"Papaw, the only conundrum I can't figure out tonight is why you picked such an easy word. Jules and I could have done way better than that." I like to cast Jules and me as a team any chance I can get. That doesn't stop Papaw from seeing an opening the size of a barn door and driving a truck through it.

"Well now, you've got a point there, Curley. I bet you *could* do better than me." Papaw sits there, his head propped up in his broad calloused hand, looking at me with those piercing blue eyes of his. "Maybe it's time you picked your own words."

Dang. The last thing I want to do is spend more time with my head in a dictionary. I don't like where this conversation is going and I need a diversion fast. That's when Jules saves the day by putting me in a different kind of trouble.

"Here, Curley. Open your present." She pulls it out from under the covers and throws it at me, where it lands squarely in my lap.

"It feels like a book," I say, stating the obvious. She has this effect on me.

"Well, duh, yeah," she says. I have this effect on her.

I pull the ribbon loose and the burlap falls away. The book has a brown leather cover but no title, and the pages are blank.

"Gosh, Jules, just what I always wanted—a book with no words. I guess you could say it's a fast read." I crack myself up, Papaw, too, but I guess Jules doesn't think it's so funny. She kicks me under the covers and just about jams my big toe.

"It's a diary, stupid." Her dimple shows up, so I know she's not really mad. "But that's not how you're going to use it." Papaw raises his left eyebrow.

"Well, that's a relief." I sigh. "You know how I hate to write." That isn't entirely true, and she knows it. I try my hand at short stories once in a while, when we have to write something for English, and I always choose Jules to be my reader.

"It's not for writing, exactly, at least not in the way you think. It's for keeping track of your papaw's words. Like keeping a dictionary."

Well, that makes me speechless, mainly because I'm not sure how much work this dictionary idea's going to entail.

Jules keeps talking about how Papaw's leaving me a legacy, like a hope chest of words, and how I should have a place to keep them. So I guess you could say Jules has saved me. No way Papaw's going to make me pick my own words now.

After Jules finishes her explanation, Papaw winks at me. Jules keeps tapping my foot under Mama's quilt like she's stepping on the gas real gentle-like. Even though it feels like she gave me homework for my birthday, I'd let her drive me just about anywhere.

"Thanks, Jules," I say. "You're a gem." She usually hates it when I say that, but she knows I have mixed feelings. She cocks her head all apologetic-like and grins back at me.

Her gift falls open, its pages all naked and white.

———

Conundrum—*noun*

1 : a kind of riddle based upon some fanciful or fantastic resemblance between things quite unlike; a puzzling question, of which the answer is or involves a pun

2 : a question to which only a conjectural answer can be made

You might think that Papaw only gives me highfalutin words, but no, he says if you leave out the fun ones, why bother? That's why *conundrum* is followed this week by *dillydally*, although it's hard to believe it's a real word. It even looks silly when you write it, like its arms and legs are sticking out all over the place, and yet it seems to like itself that way.

Papaw makes me look up my words in the dictionary we keep in the living room. We call it the Big Book or sometimes just the Book, like all the Baptists in these parts call the Bible. It sits on top of a pedestal Papaw carved out of maple wood and shaped to look like a Doric column from ancient Greece. Papaw's a woodworker and sells his furniture up in Berea, where they sell a lot of handmade stuff from Appalachian craftsmen. It's not making us rich, he says, but at least we're getting by. After seeing that mysterious handoff between him and Antsy last weekend, I've been wondering if wood-working might not be his only occupation.

I look up *dillydally* in the Big Book and write down the definition in my dictionary. Basically, it means "to waste time," like that's a bad thing. Pretty judgmental for a silly-looking word. I notice that *dillydally* is derived from the word *dally*, which means "to act playfully, *especially*"—and *especially* is italicized, as if the dictionary makers really liked that part—"to play *amorously*" (my italics).

"For cryin' out loud, Papaw, why can't I just have *dally*?"

I'm thinking of Jules, of course. Practicing *dally* would give me the perfect excuse to flirt. She'd have to dally back, since she's the one who gave me this dang dictionary in the first place. I don't recall ever begging for a word before, but this one feels important.

"Please, Papaw . . . just this once?"

"Hmmm . . ." Papaw holds a lit wooden match over his pipe and puffs until the tobacco fires red. It always looks like the eagle's head Papaw carved into the bowl of the pipe is fuming. One of his spy books lies open on his lap. As a little boy, I used to watch Papaw read, waiting for stray ash to come floating down from his pipe and set the book on fire, but it never did.

"Well, I suppose I could let you switch words this once." He clamps the pipe stem into the side of his mouth, which makes his words come out all slurpy. "But you know, Curley, I'd rather you start owning your words, rather than letting them own you."

I groan. Here comes another lesson.

"Words are like wood."

"How's that, Papaw?" When Papaw starts *philosophizing* (*p* word, last fall), it's best to go along.

"Under the proper conditions, with the right heat and moisture, wood is pliable. So are words. Meaning can change with context."

"But what does that have to do with this week's word?"

"That's just it, Curley. If you want your *dillydally* to have an amorous context, let it." His eyebrows jut up and down like they're on strings. "One person's waste of time is another person's lingering moment, if you know what I mean."

Turns out, dillydallying is something Jules and I are really good at. We'd been doing it every day on our walk to the school bus stop about a mile up the holler and didn't even know it. This morning, snowflakes are falling like a bad case of dandruff dusting everything along the trail—honeysuckle bushes, brambles, oaks, sycamores, and scraggly pines. In the summer and early fall, you can't see as far as you can spit in these woods, but now, it's like you're looking through skeletons, their jagged arms sticking out every which way against the clouded sky all the way up Red Hawk Mountain.

I join up with Jules by our special tree, an old sycamore with a hollow trunk you can crawl inside. According to Mrs. C, who knows a lot about American Indians, the sycamore is sacred to the Cherokee because it plays an important part in their creation story. When we were little, Jules and I sometimes ran away from home and hid in it. Problem was our parents always knew where to find us. Our favorite place to hang out now, though, is on the lowermost branch, which is as thick as a horse's back. That's why we call our tree Ol' Charley, after an old workhorse Jules used to ride. "Hey, Curley," Jules shouts as she comes tromping through the woods to meet up with me. Her voice sounds dry and crisp.

"Hey, Jules," I shout back. Every time I call out to her like that, I think about that Beatles song Papaw sometimes plays on his old stereo, "Hey, Jude," only I sing it in my head, "Hey, Jules."

She stomps up to me through the snow and nudges me with her backpack. The moist cloud of her breath warms my face in the frosty morning air. "Your hair looks like cinnamon and powdered sugar," she says.

"Good enough to lick?" Me being amorous. I duck my head a little in case she wants to take me up on it.

"Get real, Curley Hines. I'd rather use your head for a mop." She takes her mittened hand and shakes snow from my hair like lint. "Hey, I heard the buses are running a little late on account of the snow. Help me up on Ol' Charley, okay?"

I lace my gloved hands together like a stirrup and give her a lift up onto our special branch. Her hair brushes my face, and I smell herbal garden shampoo, something her ma makes from a secret mix of local herbs, milk, and wild honey. After she gets settled in, I pull myself up, too, facing her.

Jules gets real still up here. I know better than to talk about stuff. Her breathing slows and she peers out over the holler, watching for signs of life. Maybe this counts as dillydallying. Certainly, there are folks who would consider it a waste of time, but Jules says it's better than a good breakfast for starting the day out right.

I couldn't agree more. While she's staring out at the woods, I'm meditating on how our knees are touching and how I wish I had the guts to grab ahold of her hand.

"Curley." She hushes me like she can hear my thoughts. *"Look."*

I follow her line of sight midway up the mountain, where a magnificent buck is eating the bark off a Fraser fir. He looks up and sniffs the air. Humongous, eight-point antlers splay out behind him like a bone-white tree. I've never seen anything like him.

I lean toward Jules as my wonder deepens. "Is that a deer?"

She shakes her head almost imperceptibly. "Elk," she breathes.

It's the first one I've ever seen. Ringed with a dark brown mantle, his enormous chest radiates power; I can almost feel his heart pulsing in rhythm with mine. When he stretches his muzzle all the way out, I think he's about to gag, but then he emits this long, mournful bugle call that rolls through the holler. Jules and I look at each other in oh-my-gosh amazement as its echoes fade into the snow-packed hills.

"He seems kind of lonely," I say, rubbing my hands together for warmth.

Jules nods. "I bet he's missing his mate."

That's the only call we hear from the bull elk for the next half hour as we watch him gingerly pick his way up the mountain, nibbling at branches. Now and then, he rubs his antlers against the trunk of a tree like he's got a powerful itch. The farther up the mountain he goes, the smaller he gets in our sight, until, with one final kick and a leap, his white rump falls over the horizon, out of sight.

Jules leans back against Ol' Charley and sighs. Her breath forms a mist in the frozen air between us. I pass my hand through it to see what sticks.

Bus?

What bus?

———

Dillydally—*verb*
: to loiter or trifle; to waste time

Thwack.

"Okay, you knuckleheads, listen up!"

Everyone in fifth-period science jumps about a foot out of their seats. No matter how many times Mr. Amons begins the class this way, whacking his yardstick against the whiteboard, we're never really ready for it. You see, shots ring out for all kinds of reasons here in the hills—like for target practice or hunting season or when a second cousin from three hollers up throws a fistful of firecrackers at you on New Year's Eve. You learn to duck.

Mr. Amons runs his hand over the top of his head, like he's smoothing back hair, only there's nothing there. It's all in back, corralled into a foot-long, silver-gray ponytail. He taps the yardstick on a question he's scrawled on the board:

What do Appalachia and Noah's Ark have in common?

Mr. A calls these start-up questions "Noggin Knockers."

He says he'd rather bang our heads together to start our brains up, but the Board of Education won't allow it, so he thinks up these riddles instead.

"Anyone want to try cracking this one?" he asks in a gravelly voice, probably from chain-smoking Camel Straights. "Certainly you geniuses are awake enough by now to have begun your daily allotment of thinking—unless, of course, you ate lunch in the cafeteria." A chorus of groans rolls through the room, followed by laughter. Mr. A is off on one of his daily rants.

"What *was* that, anyway?" he says, referring to lunch. "A cardboard Frisbee soaked in tomato sauce? Do they seriously think that poor excuse for pizza has any nutritional value whatsoever? Please, someone, anyone . . . enlighten me." Mr. A's tirades are something we all look forward to, and I've got to admit, they usually get us going.

Papaw and Mr. A used to be friends. When Mr. A got out of college in the 1970s, he joined Papaw in the "War on Poverty"—something that got started back in 1964 when President Lyndon B. Johnson came down to Appalachia to have a look. Papaw had been working in construction, building schools and hospitals for over a decade, when he hired Mr. A to be on his crew. According to Papaw, that was when they were both young and *idealistic* (*i* word, fifth grade), raring to put an end to poverty and help their people. Twenty years later, I guess the war kind of petered out even though poverty hadn't. Right around that time, Papaw got laid off and Mr. A started teaching, but they were still friends.

It wasn't until sometime after Ma and little Zeb died that something broke between them, and Mr. Amons didn't come around anymore. I remember when Papaw gave me the word *irascible* when school started up last fall. I used it and Mr. Amons in a sentence together at dinner one night, and Papaw just about split a gut laughing.

"Oh, Curley," he finally said, after he soaked up the tears on his beard with his dinner napkin. "If ever they needed an illustration of the word *irascible* in Webster's Dictionary, a picture of Percy Amons would be it."

Mr. A taps the question on the board one more time. "Okay, everybody. I'm not getting any younger up here." Someone behind me mutters, "No kidding," and *thwack* goes the stick against the board. "Watch it!" he warns.

Anna Ludlow shyly raises her hand. She's one of seven Ludlow kids who live several hollers up from us. When Mama was alive, she was always bringing the family pans of grits and casseroles and such on account of how poor they are.

Not that that's unusual in these parts. More than half the kids at school are in the free lunch program.

"Miss Ludlow?" Mr. A's voice softens when he calls on her. "Pray tell, what do Appalachia and Noah's Ark have in common?"

"Ummm . . . they were both blessed by God?" Her words come out all quiet and wispy, like she looks.

"Spoken like a true, dyed-in-the-wool Baptist." Mr. A smiles at her. "And your use of the past tense is intriguing," he adds. "But unfortunately, it's not the answer I'm looking for."

Tap, tap, tap.

I try to puzzle it out. I can't help it. It's probably all those word games Papaw and I play. I can't seem to leave a stone unturned if I think there's something under it. Let's see . . . We've been focusing our studies on the local region this semester, beginning with Appalachia's flora. Maybe we're starting a new unit. Suddenly, my hand shoots up into the air, as if it has a life of its own.

"They both have a lot of animals!" I blurt out, like I'm some kind of second grader. Giggles erupt around the room, along with one outright guffaw behind me from my nemesis, Carl Jenkins. I draw my arm down slowly and hide the offending appendage under my desk.

"I mean, I'm thinking maybe we're going to be studying animals next, so that's why I said that." My face burns so hot, my skin feels like it will melt right off. When will I learn that in middle school, enthusiasm is not only *not* contagious, it's not *cool*?

Jules, who shares my lab table, gives me a sideways glance. *Don't worry*, her grin tells me, *I still like you*. That look, which only she can give, brings immediate relief to my stinging face, like how one of her ma's aloe plants soothes a burn.

"Very good, Mr. Hines." Mr. A reaches into the candy jar on his desk. "You're as close as anyone's going to get." He throws a bite-sized Snickers bar across the room at me, which I snatch from the air.

"Ah, man," I hear Carl moan behind me. I set the uneaten bar down on the lab table in plain sight, hoping he'll drool over it for the rest of the period.

"So Noah's Ark saved a whole bunch of animals from a big flood, right?" Mr. A starts pacing the room, tapping the yardstick on the tile floor like a walking cane. "Well, Appalachia saved a whole bunch of animals from another kind of disaster called the Ice Age. When the ice moved ever so glacially southward, animals migrated up into higher elevations in order to survive. Plants that had already been here for thousands of years also survived, as the wall of ice proceeded to eradicate all life in its path."

Eradicate. That's my word! Usually, I don't hear the word for the week out of anyone else's mouth besides mine and Papaw's. It's as if Papaw and Mr. Amons are in cahoots, except I know that's not possible.

"Like the Ark during the big flood," Mr. A continues, "the Appalachian Mountains during the Ice Age kept many species of animals high and dry, thereby becoming one of the most biodiverse regions in the world. Unfortunately, many of those species are now extinct, several of them only in the last hundred years.

"And why is that, my friends? Are we talking an 'act of God' here, or something else? Who's responsible for the most recent eradication of species from our mountains?" He's pointing the yardstick at us now.

"We are," we say back to him. We've heard this tirade before.

Thwack. "That's right. We are. That is, we human beings.

"The passenger pigeon. The Carolina parakeet. The ivory-billed woodpecker. The Eastern bison. The Eastern elk. And, most likely, the Eastern cougar. All gone. Wiped out. Hunted into extinction by *us*. Every last one of them."

The whole class falls silent. Mr. A leans his yardstick against the edge of his desk and stands in front of us, head hanging down, chin to chest like maybe he's praying. The image of that magnificent elk that Jules and I saw in the woods last week floats into my mind's eye, just like it emerged from the trees that day, and I can't help but raise my hand slowly.

Jules turns to me, one eyebrow raised, like she's saying, *Are you sure you want to do this* again?

Mr. A looks up. "Yes, Mr. Hines, what is it?"

"Jules and I . . . We saw one last week."

"Saw what?"

"An elk."

"Ahhh . . . an elk."

I hear a few giggles behind me. Carl leans over his lab table and whisper-spits, "Sucker."

I'm getting a sneaking suspicion I've stepped into something *excremental* (*e* word, last year—Papaw caught me saying the four-letter version one too many times, so he insisted on giving me another choice). As usual, I don't know what I'm supposed to be shaking off my boot, so I just keep walking through it.

"Yes, sir. We saw him in our holler, up in Wonder Gap. He didn't look extinct to me."

"Is that right? Hmmm . . ." He scratches his head. "Well, it looks like you found your next research project, Mr. Hines, or rather, it found you."

"What planet are you from, Hines?" Carl blurts out, his cronies laughing along with him.

Thwack.

"Watch your trap, Mr. Jenkins," Mr. A says, "or you're the one who will find yourself without a planet, if you catch my drift."

Carl leans back in his chair. "Awww, Mr. A, I was just trying to point out—"

"And I was just about to point out that the Carolina parakeet just became your next project."

Carl drops his chair forward with a bang. The whole class is laughing at *him* now.

Mr. Amons makes a grand sweep of the classroom with his stick, like it's some kind of magic wand that will turn us into good students, or maybe he's wishing we'd all disappear.

"In case the rest of you knuckleheads think you're immune from this assignment, think again. Each of you is going to team up with one other person, pick an extinct animal, and then develop a presentation that will have the rest of us weeping in the aisles that it's gone. You've got the rest of the marking period to get it together and it counts for a major part of your grade, so it better be good."

Thwack. Thwack.

Jules and I look over at each other and smile. There are few comforts you can count on in middle school, but knowing that your best friend will always pick you to be her science partner is one of them.

Toward the end of the period, Mr. A gives us some time to meet with our partners to discuss strategy. Jules thinks the elk we saw wasn't an Eastern elk, but another kind of elk transplanted from somewhere else. Her ma told her they were dropped off to the north of us and are now making their way into our area. This isn't nearly as cool as finding the last remaining Eastern elk on earth, but it has me curious. How do you transplant an elk, anyway?

Jules and I are the last ones to leave the room. We're stuffing our books into our backpacks when this new guy comes shuffling up to Mr. A's desk and hands him a pass.

"Ah, Mr. James David Tiverton III, I presume. I was expecting you a little earlier. Like for class, for instance."

"Sorry," the kid mutters, not offering any excuse. "And it's JD."

"Ah . . . of *course*."

Mr. A signs the slip as he looks over his gold-rimmed reading glasses and stares straight into the new boy's eyes, or rather, eye. The kid's straight, jet-black hair sweeps over his other eye, blotting out half his face, like one of those bad boys I've seen in the movies. And by "bad boys," I mean the ones girls usually fall for, which has me looking at Jules to see what she sees.

She leans in so close that her cheek brushes my hair, and for a minute I forget that anyone else is in the room. "That's the new coal boss's son Celia May was telling me about," she whispers, and I know that my first hunch is correct. News of this guy's coming has already zapped through the rumor mill.

"I see this is the second time you've taken seventh-grade science." Mr. A hands him back the pass. "Maybe you can teach the rest of us a thing or two, seeing as you're older and . . . I'm assuming . . . wiser . . . than the first time around." The kid shrugs and stuffs the slip into his front jeans pocket.

Great. The only thing worse than a bad boy is an *older* bad boy, and a tall, dark, and broody one at that. I glance at Jules to see if I'm right. Yup. Her eyes are most definitely superglued onto this JD fella, and I'm not liking it one bit. I would like nothing better right now than to eradicate bad boys from the planet.

"Good news, you two." Mr. A is speaking to me and Jules now, and I can't imagine what "good" he could possibly mean. "Since everyone else in the class has already teamed up, there's only one option I can see for our new friend here." With that, he slaps this Tiverton guy on the back like he's some kind of prize or something.

"Meet your new partner."

———————

Eradicate—*verb*

1 : to pluck up by the roots; to root up

2 : to root out; to destroy utterly; to extirpate

"But, Papaw, she's so doggone blind to who this JD character really is." I pull the mask covering my nose and mouth down to my chin so he can hear me.

I've been helping him rip wood for a new cabinet he's making, catching planks of cherry as he runs them through the table saw. It really kicks up the dust. Our conversation about Jules and the new boy at school has had its fits and starts, like almost every conversation I've ever had with Papaw here in his woodshop. It used to irritate me, but now I'm glad for it. It gives me time to think about my comebacks, which, when you're trying to make a point with Papaw, is a down-right necessity.

Papaw takes the plank from me and brushes off the shavings, looking it up and down, like how I caught Jules looking at JD when he was reaching for a book on a library shelf. His T-shirt crept up as he reached, showing his bare back along with the ribbed waistband of his paisley boxer shorts. I stared at Jules staring at him and it just about drove me crazy.

"Well now, Curley, I expect Jules knows what she's doing. Besides, what terrible thing could happen between the two of them working on a science project, especially with you watching their every move?" Even through Papaw's scratched-up safety glasses, I can see the twinkle in his eyes, which really ticks me off.

"It's what could happen between the two of them when I'm *not* there that worries me, Papaw. You should see how she looks at him—all googly-eyed and all." Honestly, do I have to spell it out for him?

"Oh, I see." He taps the narrow edge of the plank three times on the cement floor, knocking the sawdust off, and leans on it. "This is more serious than I thought."

"*Thank you,*" I say facetiously, which you might think is the word for the week, but it's not. I learned it from Mr. A, who says it a lot when he fools us into thinking he's dead serious.

Now that I seem to have Papaw's full attention, I hardly know what to do with it. I turn on the Shop-Vac and start sucking up sawdust, one of my jobs. Papaw stands there patiently, waiting for me to finish. The silence that remains after the vacuum shuts down feels heavy with anticipation, like how the mountains feel in early spring.

"So what's really going on, Curley?" Papaw finally says, staring at me with his eagle eyes. "I mean, with *you*?"

His cool gaze burns right through my chest, like he has this superpower that can see straight through to my heart. I know I can't hide from that look, nor do I really want to. His seeing me like that makes me want to find the truth and tell it. If only I knew what it was.

"Try starting with what's on top," he says, placing the cherry plank on his workbench to sand. I hop onto a stool and lean back against the pegboard wall. All I can think about is Jules staring at JD's boxer shorts.

"For starters, Papaw, she knows what kind of underwear he wears," I say. "No girl should know that."

"Hmmm . . . that does sound kind of personal."

"Well, *yeah*. She doesn't even know I wear Jockeys."

"Now, that's a relief."

"No kidding, Papaw. What if she starts knowing more about him than she knows about me?" That day at the library working on our report, Jules jabbered at JD like she used to jabber at me. I felt like one of those cast-off pieces of wood Papaw throws on his scrap pile and later burns for kindling.

"Three can be hard," he says as he flips off his safety glasses and tosses them on the bench. "Real hard. I've been the odd man out a time or two myself."

Papaw shakes the sawdust out of his hair, like he's shaking off a memory. "Seems like it would take years for Jules to know JD like she knows you, though. What's personal goes a lot deeper than knowing the brand of someone's underwear." He picks up the hand sander and runs the block along the wood in long strokes. Whoooosh, whoooosh.

Usually, Papaw's words comfort me, but all the wisdom in the world can't make this uneasy feeling go away. With every pass Papaw makes across the wood, I feel my stomach tighten.

"But why does she even *like* the guy?" I yell over Papaw's sanding. He freezes midswipe and stands, listening. "I mean, he seems kind of creepy. It's not as if he's even nice to her. Like when she dropped her books on the way out of the library, he didn't even stop to help her pick them up. And then when I did, she didn't even thank me. She was too busy rushing off to catch up with Mr. JD Tiverton the *Third*. Honestly, Papaw, what good does it do being a good guy when the bad guys always get the girls?"

Papaw starts shaking all over, hunched over his sander, like he's having some kind of attack. He's shaking so hard that sawdust drops in clouds from his leather apron. I'm about to reach for the phone hanging by the door to call 911 when he busts out laughing in these huge, gulping guffaws.

"I swear, Curley, my dear boy. I don't think I'm ready for this."

"Not ready for what, Papaw?"

He chugs about half a liter of water from a Ball jar he keeps on a ledge. When he's drained it of every last drop, he slams it down on the workbench. "Not ready for you to grow up, that's *what*. Not ready for you to be navigating this crazy, mixed-up maze we call adulthood, that's *what*." He spits his *t*'s out like paper wads.

Under his breath, so softly I almost can't hear him, he says, "I don't know what I was thinking when we lost your ma and little Zeb to that river of sludge, but for some reason I thought—I *thought*—I could handle this." He starts rubbing his upper arm like it's got a terrible ache. "Not that I had any choice."

Whoa. All of a sudden my chest feels all tight and airless like the inside of that Shop-Vac packed with wood shavings. I never thought about Papaw not being here with me. I mean, I never thought he might have something else he'd rather be doing.

41

Papaw ambles over and puts his arm around my shoulders. "Never you mind, son. Never you mind the crazy ramblings of a tired old man, you hear? Besides, it's about time you found out how *fallible* I really am."

Fallible. Yup, that's our word for the week, and I'm really starting to hate it. If someone like Papaw can be less than what I thought they were or weak or bad or downright wrong, then who can I count on? My stomach churns like when I stood there looking down into my mama's grave. Dark. Hollow. Empty.

Papaw grabs a piece of carved wood from a shoe box on the windowsill and hands it to me. It's a spurtle, a funny name for a Scottish stirring stick that he sells at art fairs in the summer along with his furniture and wooden bowls. We call it our "thinking wood." I hold the flat stick in the palm of my hand and rub my thumb up and down its silky-smooth surface. Immediately, I feel the muscles around my stomach ease.

Papaw's two strong hands grip each of my shoulders as he peers at me from under his bushy white brows. "Look here, Curley. I can tell you're in a tough place about Jules and this JD guy, and I'm not sayin' it's going to be easy. I wish I could tell you that the good guy always gets the girl, but I can't."

"Wait a minute, Papaw. Are you saying Jules could actually wind up going for this guy?" I feel like cracking that spurtle right over my knee. "Do you mean she's just as fallible as you are?"

"Heaven forbid." He laughs softly. "In this case, I'd say Jules is being *gullible*—your word for next week, incidentally. The difference between the two words isn't always obvious."

"Right, Papaw." Just what I need, another word to help me express what a miserable life I'm having.

"These are hard words to learn," Papaw says, as if reading my mind. "Even harder to see in ourselves, if you catch my drift."

Actually, I don't, but my head's hurting and I tell Papaw I've got homework to do. Before I get out the door of the shop, however, he asks me to run to the house and get his bottle of heart pills. He's rubbing his left arm again.

"Sure, Papaw. Be right back."

I rummage through a pile of receipts on Papaw's dresser, searching for the small plastic bottle of pills I often see on the table by his reading chair. There are days he pops those pills like Jules pops Tic Tacs on the way to school when she's forgotten to brush her teeth.

I find the bottle under a receipt from Home Depot and am about to take off back to the woodshop when, next to an old framed photo of my grandparents on their wedding day, I see a small, padded white envelope. Figuring it's the one Antsy handed Papaw, my curiosity gets the best of me. I pick it up and the flap falls open, revealing a wad of hundred-dollar bills.

The word *payoff* zaps through my mind again, only this time it's blinking neon. But payoff for *what*? What kind of shady deal has Papaw made with the coal company? It's got to be shady, right? Why else would it be cash? In hundred-dollar bills? And as far as I can tell, a lot of them. I count them. Twenty-three. And there were probably more.

I'm feeling hollow again, like I don't even know what kind of pit I'm looking into.

———

Fallible—*adjective*
: liable to fail, mistake, or err; liable to deceive or to be deceived

G

It's two weeks into our science project on Eastern elk, and Jules and JD have decided we're meeting at JD's house to do more research. JD says his Internet connection is probably better than ours because he lives at the top of a mountain and not in a holler like the rest of us. I guess JD's pa bought the former coal boss's house and spent some big money on it.

My house is out, of course, since we don't even have Internet, much less a computer, but I wasn't going to say that. Jules didn't mention it, either, although I'm pretty sure Internet service was the last thing on her mind. She plumb lit up after science class on Friday when JD offered his house for our next meeting.

"Oh, JD," she cooed, "you're the bomb."

The *bomb*?

"Since when did you start talking like a city kid?" I ask her on the bus that afternoon on the forty-five-minute ride home from school. She's been staring out the window at the blur of hills and hollers rushing by and chewing on the end of a strand of hair. I used to think it was cute, but now for some reason it's annoying me.

"What do you mean?" she snaps.

"I mean, calling JD 'the bomb' and all. It's not like he's going to blow up in your face." Honestly, I'm trying to lighten things up, but she's staring holes in me.

"Just because I use a word that's not in your dictionary suddenly means I'm a fake?"

"Well, no . . . not exactly. I just wondered . . . I mean . . . I never heard you talk like that before, that's all." Not the most brilliant comeback, but then, Jules and I rarely fight. "Besides, you gave me that dictionary, remember?"

Jules rolls her eyes, pulls a book out of her backpack, and slaps it open on her lap. "Well, JD talks like that, and I happen to think it's cool."

These last words of hers sting like a passel of yellow jackets knocked from their nest, but it's her silence for the rest of the way home that hurts even worse.

Today on the way to JD's house, Jules is all palsy-walsy with me again, as if our argument never happened. When Mrs. Cavanaugh, Jules's ma, pulls up to our front stoop in her old, rusted-out Jeep, Jules hops in back with me as soon as I get in.

The first thing that hits me is that Jules doesn't smell like Jules. It's like a whole truckload of lilacs or gardenias gets dumped into the Jeep with her, and I resist the urge to hold my nose. You might think I'm exaggerating, but if a smell can have a kick to it, this one would send you clear over the mountains. I decide to keep that to myself.

"Gee, Jules, you sure do smell nice."

Rather than hitting me on the arm like she usually does when I give her a compliment, she tilts her head to one side and blushes. *Blushes!* I've never been able to get Jules to blush at anything, and Lord knows I've tried.

I catch Mrs. C looking at us in the rearview mirror. Her eyes are smiling, but for the life of me, I don't know why. This isn't the Jules I know. I'm not even sure I like her. Besides, she keeps talking about JD this and JD that, like he's her favorite subject. We'll probably meet his dad, she says, but his mom is still up in Indiana waiting for their house to sell.

"JD thinks they may be getting a divorce, but don't say anything," she tells me. "He's kind of touchy about it." As if I have any interest in the Tivertons' personal lives whatsoever.

The slow, winding climb up JD's paved driveway, up his very own mountain to his very own family mansion, reminds me of how a movie sometimes starts out with a panoramic view before it zooms in on the movie star. And there he is, in all of his bad-boy finest, standing on the fieldstone steps of his stone-walled castle—black jeans, black T-shirt, black stringy hair, hands in his tight front pockets, all casual and nonchalant like the mansion behind him is some shack in the woods somewhere with some skimpy view of a landfill and not this amazing scene of rolling blue hills as far as the eye can see.

I can almost feel Jules's heart pounding next to me as she breaks into a smile as wide as her face and waves at him through the car window. He lifts the fingers of a pocketed hand slightly, and the ends of his mouth twitch like he's trying to grin.

"Look there, Jules, he's really glad to see us."

Jules ignores my sarcasm, probably doesn't even hear it. She grabs her backpack and is out of the car, slamming the door in my face like I'm not even there.

"Jules!" her ma yells after her, and then looks back at me. "Sorry, Curley. I don't know what's gotten into that girl."

"I do," I say under my breath as I slide out the door. "See you later, Mrs. C."

I feel like I'm entering enemy territory, this being the coal boss's house and all. Even Mrs. C kidded us about keeping our eyes out for shady dealings, which made me think of Papaw, of course. After JD first showed up at school, I heard Jules beg her ma to take the I ♥ MOUNTAINS bumper sticker off her car, as if he might refuse to be her science partner if he saw it.

"Who doesn't love mountains?" Mrs. C had replied, all innocent-like, but Jules and I both know she's attended her share of protests in Frankfort against the coal industry. Heck, we've helped her make the signs.

"Hey, Curley." JD greets me at the door as if we're pals or something and ushers me through the marble-tiled entryway. "Jules is already in the den. My dad's got a fire going. We're going to chill in there."

"Okay, sure," I say, keeping my thoughts about chilling by the fire to myself.

The Tivertons' den is almost the size of our school cafeteria, with mahogany paneling lining the walls in a diagonal pattern. There's enough wood in a single wall for Papaw to make an entire bedroom set. Overstuffed couches and armchairs surround a fieldstone fireplace at the center of the room with a big-screen TV over the mantel. At the west end, an entire wall of glass showcases a panoramic view of the Appalachians.

It looks like the Tivertons love mountains, too.

As JD and I head toward the fireplace, I notice Jules has her jacket off and is spreading her books out on a large, round coffee table. Instead of the oversized flannel shirt she usually wears on weekends, she's wearing a soft, light green sweater. JD slips onto the couch next to her and opens up his laptop, sneaking glances in her direction as he waits for it to boot up. The only logical place for me to sit is in a chair across from them, and I remember what Papaw said: Three can be hard.

Surprisingly, once we get going on our project, ideas start snap-cracking between us. Papaw would say we've got *synergy* (*s* word, last year), but JD says we're *sick*, which I'm guessing is a good thing. I'd ask, but I feel like I should already know what it means.

By the time we're ready to wrap things up, we've divvied up the work. That is, JD and Jules have decided they'll research the Eastern elk together and what caused its extinction. That leaves me researching the elk that are living here now, since I brought it up in class and Mr. A jumped all over it. I feel like a third wheel, what with the two of them pairing up like that, but I'm scrambling to take the high road about it. Besides, our work session has gone far better than I ever imagined.

"No slackers in this group," JD says, extending the flat of his hand across the coffee table for a high five, something that always makes me nervous. I raise my hand to slap his and miss. We try again and I catch his little finger. So much for synergy.

I hate to admit it, though. I'm actually starting to like the guy.

Until he invites Jules up to his room.

I'm taking a few last-minute notes off JD's laptop when Jules says she wants to see some old photographs of Eastern elk JD previously found on the Internet.

"Come on." JD takes Jules's hand and tugs her up from the couch. "We can find it on my desktop upstairs. The graphics are better there, anyway." Jules blushes for the second time today, the skin on her neck flaring pink.

According to Webster's, *gullible* means "easily deceived," and when it comes to Jules, it's the "easy" part that's got me worried. Papaw says that words are mirrors and that's where their power lies, but doggone it, I'm not the one being easy here, that's for sure.

As Jules follows JD out of the den, she looks back over her shoulder.

"Be right back, Curley."

"Sure," I say. "Take your time."

They're up there for what feels like hours, though the grandfather clock in the corner has chimed only once on the quarter hour since they left. A man in faded jeans and a red Indiana University sweatshirt comes into the den and grabs the TV remote off the coffee table.

"Hey there. You must be one of JD's buddies from school." He extends his hand. "I'm JD's dad, Jim Tiverton."

"Mr. Tiverton." I nod. "Curley Hines."

"Nice to meet you, Curley." He slaps the remote against his thigh. "Hines . . . I don't recall seeing that name on our roster. I was just going over our list of employees the other day with my general manager. You don't have any family working in the mines, do you?"

"No, sir." I can barely get the words out. "Not anymore."

The word *hate* isn't a helpful word, Papaw says, but it's what I'm feeling now as I think about what this man in front of me represents. Carl Jenkins's dad is fond of saying, "Coal keeps the lights on," but as far as I can tell, coal has knocked the lights out for good on a lot of folks, including my family.

"My daddy died in the mines, sir." It's all I can do to keep from spitting on his oriental rug.

"I see." Mr. Tiverton carefully sets the remote down on the arm of the couch and faces me. "I'm sorry, Curley."

As much as I want to dislike this man, I can see that he means it. It's the first time anyone connected to coal mining has said those words to me or anyone I love. For some reason that I really, really hate, tears spring into my eyes. To counter the effect, I think about that envelope of money I found on Papaw's dresser and how angry it made me feel. Maybe I can get to the bottom of this shady deal after all.

"You might know my grandfather, John Weaver?" I try to make my words come out all smooth and casual-like as I swallow back the tears draining down my throat. "I think he's a friend of coal."

Now *I* feel like the traitor, bending words to suit my purpose, like Papaw bends wood. Papaw would never say he's a friend of coal, although he doesn't say much about it one way or another. If my words get to the truth, though, isn't that enough to make them right?

"Ah . . . Weaver . . . Yes, I *do* recognize that name." Mr. Tiverton considers me carefully, and then a sad look falls across his face. It's a familiar look. Someone has told him about my family, most likely Antsy Martin. Just then, JD and Jules come into the den, laughing and cutting up. I look for signs of dishevelment, but Jules's hair looks as messy as ever, so it's hard to tell.

"Uh, Jules, this is my old man." JD gestures toward Mr. Tiverton. "Old Man, this is Jules."

"Gee, JD, what a lovely introduction." Mr. Tiverton shakes Jules's hand. "Please forgive my son. He learned his manners from his mother."

Jules laughs, but JD stares darts at his dad.

"Hey, guys . . ." Mr. Tiverton ignores his son's glare. "I hear you're studying elk for your science class. There's a herd of elk up on one of our mining sites north of here. The state park runs elk tours up there. I can get the three of you signed up for one, if you want. What do you say?"

JD continues to fume at his father, and I'm still trying to work out what Antsy might have told Mr. Tiverton about Papaw, but Jules is all over the invitation like a bee on a clump of clover.

"Gee, Mr. Tiverton, that's a super idea," she gushes. "I say we do it." She turns to me and JD. "Guys? How 'bout it?"

"Whatever," JD says.

"Sure." I try to sound enthusiastic. Truth be told, I'm kind of worn out after worrying about Jules up in JD's room and then heaping all that hate onto JD's dad. I mean, he *did* say he was sorry for my daddy and all, which I really do appreciate, and he really seems to want to help us with our project.

Jules's ma is waiting for us out in the driveway, but before I can follow Jules out the door, Mr. Tiverton takes me aside.

"Curley, give my best to your grandfather, okay? Tell him . . . Tell him I think he's got a fine grandson and we'll talk soon."

About what? I want to ask, but Jules and her ma are waiting. I leave the Tivertons' feeling more confused than ever.

Maybe they aren't the enemy after all.

———

Gullible—*adjective*

: easily deceived, overly trustful

H

The next day at breakfast, Papaw gives me *hutzpah*. He says it's a Yiddish word that usually starts with *c*, but that the Big Book allows *hutzpah* with an *h* as a variant, and besides, he says, "This won't wait for the next *c* word to come along.

"Seems like you need *hutzpah* right here and now, Curley," he says over his grits and sausage. "I can tell you're all shaken up about something, like a bottle of Coke ready to burst."

He's right, of course, and he's half the reason. Between him and Jules, I don't know who to trust anymore. And worse, I don't know who to talk to.

The problem with being a bottled-up Coke is that you have to wait for someone else to pop the cap; the pressure's simply too great inside and you can't pop it yourself. So all I do is sit there. Not eating. Not talking. Just stirring my grits and stewing, thinking about the secret that Papaw's keeping from me about all that coal money. Papaw's fond of saying that we have no secrets in this house, but here he is keeping the biggest one of all.

"Did something happen at JD's house yesterday?" Papaw leans back in his chair and studies me. "Seems like you've been angry about something ever since you got back."

I jerk my head up from my plate. It's like he's poking me in the ribs, and I want to poke him back.

"Come on, Curley. Say what's on your mind. I can take it."

"Can you, Papaw?" I stare daggers at him.

Papaw juts his chin out and jabs at the air between us with his fists, like he used to play-fight with me when I was five. I pound the end of my fork on the table.

"For crying out loud, Papaw, I'm not a little kid anymore." I rarely raise my voice against him, so we're both pretty shocked, but doggone it, he asked for it. "And I'm not stupid, either."

"Why in the world would I think *that*?"

"Something's going on between you and the coal company, Papaw, and you think you can hide it from me. Some kind of money exchange. Something *shady*."

"Oh, *that*." His shoulders slump.

"Yeah, that. And while I'm at it, Mr. Tiverton says hi. You know, your old buddy Jim?" I hardly recognize my own voice.

"He says to tell you that you've got a nice boy here and that you guys will talk soon."

"He said that?" He looks up expectantly.

"Yeah, Papaw. Those were his words, and he talked like maybe I might know something, which I *don't*, because you won't tell me."

Papaw's the silent one now, so I keep yammering away.

"I found money on your dresser the other day when I came in to get your pills. That money came from Antsy Martin, didn't it? And I wasn't supposed to see it, was I? But why, Papaw? What's going on?"

Without looking up at me, Papaw throws his napkin down and pushes his chair back from the table, wood scraping wood. Turning toward the sink, he says, "Sorry, Curley, I'm not ready to tell you that right now. These are adult matters you shouldn't have to worry about."

"But it's too late, Papaw. I *am* worried. It's got me worried *sick*." I'm pleading now, drained of any *hutzpah* I might have had.

Papaw pours himself another cup of coffee. Leaning against the kitchen counter, he takes what looks like a painful sip, or maybe that grimace has something to do with me.

Either way, I can tell he's thinking about what I just said. I hold my breath.

"Well, I guess this is what I get for giving you a word like *hutzpah*, eh?" He laughs softly. "I've got to give it to you, Curley, it takes guts to confront me like this."

I want to say, *You asked for it*, but he's already admitting that.

"Want some coffee?" Papaw lifts the old percolator off the stove. I nod and he grabs a mug from a hook. I don't usually drink coffee, but his offer feels important. No cream.

"Come on, Curley. Let's go out to the porch and talk to our mountain."

This is code for having a family meeting, and I couldn't be more excited and terrified at the same time. Now that the truth is about to be revealed, I wonder: Do I really want to hear it?

There's a raw cold hanging over everything, it being late February and all. Clumps of snow still dot the backwoods. Papaw settles into his rocker while I ease onto the porch swing, toss an old army blanket over my legs to ward off the chill, and wait. Both of us sip at our coffee as we watch the eastern sun spread its golden rays behind Red Hawk Mountain.

"You're right, Curley," Papaw finally says. "It's time you knew what was going on."

His words send a rush of adrenaline through me, like I sometimes feel at night when I hear rustling in the woods outside my bedroom window and I know it's something big.

"After your ma and little Zeb died, Barkley Coal was scared to death that I was going to sue them in a court of law. Lord knows I had a busload of lawyers calling me every day, jabbering at me to do just that. All of those yokels were saying a lawsuit could be worth millions of dollars, if it went our way."

Did he say *millions*? As in, more than one? Every time I move the swing even a hair's breadth, the chains groan, so I put a foot down to steady it. Papaw has stopped rocking, too.

"What they didn't say was how long it would take or how much of our lives would be consumed in the process. These things can take *years*. A company like Barkley has time and money on their side. Any judgment found in our favor would most certainly be appealed again and again, which, of course, would mean more time, more money in legal fees, more years of a life I never planned on spending in a courtroom. By the time it was settled, you'd probably be out of school."

I'm thinking about how many houses I could buy after I graduate with *millions* of dollars, when Papaw pulls out his pipe and starts loading it with tobacco.

"That doesn't even begin to touch the politics—how people would feel pressured to take sides, for and against. When folks depend upon mining for their livelihood, which a lot of them do around these parts, they can do and say all kinds of crazy things when they think you're going against Big Coal. I didn't want you to be caught in the middle of all that."

My jaw aches, I've been clenching it so tight.

"So when Antsy Martin came to me with an offer from Mr. Barkley to settle out of court without lawyering up, I had to give it a lot of thought. Honestly, Curley, you were my first priority. After losing all of your people in the seven short years of your life, you needed stability above all else. So I made the choice to settle with Big Coal to keep Big Coal out of our lives."

"But what about—"

"Curley, let me finish."

For spite, I think, he takes a full minute to light his pipe. Striking a wooden matchstick with his thumbnail, he pulls the flame into the packed tobacco with long, slow puffs until the bowl glows red. The smoke that fills the air between us reminds me of the bonfires Mama used to build with applewood after pruning our orchard. The smell of Papaw's tobacco never fails to sadden and comfort me all at the same time.

"So you see, Curley, there was a payoff, but there was nothing shady about it. Thanks to Barkley Coal, you now have a college fund, and we get a monthly sum that meets our bills and a little more. What I make from the woodshop helps, too, but without the coal money, we'd be living in a city like Lexington or Cincinnati, where your Aunt Gertie lives, because I'd need to find a good-paying job. Lord knows there's nothing like that around here.

"If I'd made the choice to sue, we'd still not have our millions, if ever; we'd be living away from the mountains; you wouldn't have Jules; and who knows, we might not even have each other. What's that worth, Curley? What's all that worth?"

My throat gets all dry and tight just thinking about everything I'd be missing, and I swallow hard. I could see his point.

"The cash was the one thing I insisted on," Papaw continues. "I wanted them paying me in cold, hard cash. I wanted them going to the bank and pulling out that money and handing it to me personally every blasted month, in the hopes they'd think about the lives that no longer walk these hills because of their shoddy sludge pond. It's a little thing, but I didn't want to make it any easier for them, when it hasn't been easy for us."

Just then, a mama deer and her speckled fawn appear in the woods through the morning fog. It's like one of those Magic Eye pictures where suddenly a figure jumps out at you from a page of jumbled dots. The mama deer keeps her eye on us as I think about how my life might have been different these past few years if Papaw had been all tied up in a fight. And then, when I think about all those heart pills he takes, I can't imagine what it might have done to *him*. Still, with so much at stake, I feel cheated of something.

"Why didn't you tell me about all this, Papaw? You're always sayin' we're a team. I feel kind of fooled with all this going on and me not knowing."

"I can see how you'd feel that way." He exhales a long stream of smoke. "I guess I wanted to protect you, Curley. I wanted your life to go on as normal as possible, even though there was nothing normal about losing your closest kin."

Something snaps in the woods. The deer and fawn startle and bound out of sight.

"Down deep, though?" Papaw sits with his pipe resting on his knee, staring off at the mountain. "I was keeping it from you for another reason, one I'm not very proud of."

"What was that, Papaw?"

"Curley, my boy, I was plumb tired—worn out from grief and the thought of raising a boy to manhood. I'm ashamed to say it, but in some ways, I just caved in."

This latest revelation jolts me more than all of the preceding news combined. I can't imagine my papaw caving in or being ashamed of anything.

He taps down the smoldering tobacco in his pipe with the tip of his finger. "My old friend, your teacher, the irascible Mr. Amons, was quick to judge me on that. Oh, *man*. He and I had many a lively discussion, if you can call them that, on this very porch at night after you'd gone to bed."

"He wanted you to sue the pants off Big Coal?" That part isn't hard to guess, Mr. A being an old hippie and all.

"Of course he did. Said they had it coming. Said it was my civic duty. Heck, he said it was my *sacred* duty, to God and country and all that." Papaw snaps another match. It flares and he gets the bowl of tobacco glowing again.

"What did you say to that, Papaw?" I'm imagining Mr. A

sitting on this very swing attacking the porch railing with his yardstick. *Thwack. Thwack.*

"I told him I had a familial duty above all others."

"Familial?"

"Duty to family. Duty to you."

"What did he say to that?"

"I recall it was something I'd rather not repeat."

"Oh."

"Yeah, *oh.*" Papaw laughs, spewing smoke in all directions. "That ornery ol' coot doesn't mince words. I've got to admit, though, his verdict still rings in my ears." He hangs his head, chin to chest, like he's listening to Mr. A all over again. "After all is said and done, maybe I lacked the hutzpah to fight."

This last bit makes my skin crawl. I hate seeing Papaw like this, so I try to steer the conversation to a place where we can shut the door on it.

"What happens now, Papaw? Now that Mr. Tiverton has taken over?"

"Ah, there's the rub. My agreement was with Barkley Coal, you see. And since we settled it all with a handshake, there's nothing that says the new company has to honor it. Barkley's been mining these mountains for over fifty years. I never thought about them leaving. When Antsy came to tell me about the sale, I didn't think we had a snowball's chance in heck that Tiverton would keep the payments up. That is, until you told me about that little exchange you had with him yesterday."

My thoughts shoot back to that moment by the door, how Mr. Tiverton seemed to know something about me, how before that he had said he was sorry for my daddy's death. Surely he knows about Ma and little Zeb, too. Maybe I helped put a face to all that pain.

"I wish this conversation could have waited until after I talk with him." Papaw stood up from his rocker and stretched. "I don't want you to fret about it, you hear? No matter what, you and I are going to come out shining, like the sun when it climbs over Red Hawk Mountain."

As if on cue, the whole holler lights up. A blinding light glistens off the morning dew. I think about Papaw and all he's been holding, keeping all of this coal business to himself for the longest time. Maybe that *c* in front of *chutzpah* stands for courage, silent like a mountain.

"One more thing, Curley." Papaw reaches for my hand to help me out of the swing. "Part of my agreement with Barkley—and I'm sure it would be the same with Tiverton, too—was never to speak out against them. That would extend to you."

I think about JD's dad in his Indiana sweatshirt getting ready to watch a basketball game, and I feel my hate for Big Coal losing its edge now that it has a face. Papaw hangs his arm over my shoulder as we take one last look at our mountain before going in.

"No problem," I say.

———

Hutzpah (from the Hebrew, *chutzpah*)—*noun*
: bravery, often in the face of tremendous odds; boldness; audacity

"Hey, y'all. Whitney Calhoun here, but you can call me Ranger Whit. You must be the Tiverton party. Welcome aboard!"

It's 6:30 on a cold and rainy Saturday morning when Jules, JD, and I pile into a rickety, converted school bus to join the elk tour. The ranger's voice is so cheerful it hurts.

True to his word, Mr. Tiverton has prearranged our meet-up with the tour at an abandoned gas station several miles outside the state park. He even drove us here in his Cadillac SUV. I don't mean to put on airs or anything, but leaving his Caddy for this drafty old bus? I get the feeling I'll be longing for heated seats by the end of the day.

As we file past him, Ranger Whit turns and addresses the rest of his passengers, a sea of mostly gray and balding heads. "Hey, everybody, meet Kentucky's future park rangers!"

I hear JD mutter, "Over your dead body," as he follows me and Jules up the narrow center aisle. To counter the moodiness of his late arrivals or perhaps to embarrass us further, Ranger Whit says, "Hey, you guys can earn a ranger badge today if you stay alert!"

As the three of us squeeze into the last remaining seat at the back of the bus, our tour guide crunches the bus into gear and pulls out of the abandoned parking lot. Soon we're bouncing our way to what he's calling an "active and reclaimed mining site" about fifteen miles or so into the hills to get a good look at a local elk herd. I say "bouncing" because our location over the rear wheel well has us riding every bump, hump, and pothole like we're roped to a bucking bronco. Add to that the noxious smell of exhaust leaking in from some rusty hole somewhere, and my morning grits are lumping up in my gut something awful.

By some miracle of fate, I'm sitting *between* Jules and JD, who, I might as well tell you, have become a hot item at school. Some days it makes me sicker than others to see them holding hands in the hall or JD leaning into Jules at her locker, but I'm starting to take the long view with Papaw's help. I already know that JD wants out of Kentucky something fierce; he's told me as much when we're working on our project during study hall and Jules is in French. He says not to tell

Jules because she hates to hear him talking about it. I want to tell her, but I don't. I figure I'm staying in these mountains forever, so I can wait JD out.

Still, I wasn't exactly looking forward to this day, feeling like a tagalong and all. Add to that the miserable weather and I'd much rather be home helping Papaw in his shop or playing harmonica up in my room. Sitting in the middle like this, though, has me thinking. Maybe they're not tied at the hip like I thought. Maybe Jules is having second thoughts already. Maybe, just maybe, Jules would rather be sitting by me, us being lifelong friends and all.

JD pulls out his cell phone, which has a skull and cross-bones on the back cover. He's wearing a pair of thin black gloves cut off at the tips so he can text. I swear his thumbs are faster than greased lightning. He taps SEND, spits out some swear words, and then taps again harder.

Jules lets out a big huff and leans over me. "Give it up, JD. How many times do I have to tell you, there's no coverage out here?"

He glares back at her. A black leather band tooled with silver studs slips down his wrist. He shakes it back over the cuff of his leather jacket and keeps on tapping.

"He's obsessed with getting in touch with his buddies back in Indiana," she says. "Like they're his lifeline or something, like he's going to die without them."

That's when it hits me like a truckload of manure. They're having their first tiff. A low-grade current of dark energy is streaming between them, and I'm smack-dab in the middle of it. *Great.*

I decide to back out of their little drama, seeing how I'm not even supposed to be in it. Besides, I know better than to make a comment, for or against, when Jules is in a funk like this, so I lean back and pretend to catch some shut-eye. I hear JD shove his phone back into his pack and sigh. About fifteen minutes later, Ranger Whit comes on the intercom to fill us in on what we're about to see.

"A little way up this hill here, we're going to turn onto a mining road as we enter property owned by the Tiverton Coal Corporation. This site recently changed hands, so it's kind of a big deal that the park service still has permission to drive over their land."

I nudge JD, expecting him to be proud of his pa for his generosity and all, but he just smirks. I'm hoping Mr. Tiverton shows that same generosity to Papaw and me when Papaw goes to talk to him next week.

"Keep your eyes open, y'all. Elk like to hang out on mountaintop removal sites such as the one we're about to see, where the land has been reclaimed. The mining company is responsible for resurfacing the mining site after it's been stripped of coal, filling in some of the valleys with the leftover rock and debris and then planting new vegetation. Turns out, elk love these new grassy plateaus, so you'll often see them congregating there."

We turn onto the gravel mining road. NO TRESPASSING signs are posted everywhere. The intercom clicks on again as Ranger Whit continues his lecture. I should probably be taking notes, but the drone of the bus engine is making me sleepy.

"As some of you probably know, elk disappeared from Kentucky around the time of the Civil War, mostly due to overhunting. Starting in 1997, however, just over fifteen hundred elk from out west were transplanted to eastern Kentucky over a five-year period. With no natural predators and a ninety percent breeding rate, those first elk herds have grown to over ten thousand. Isn't that something?"

"Wow," JD says under his breath as he elbows me. "That's a lot of you-know-what." And I just about bust a gut trying not to laugh. Jules rolls her eyes at both of us.

"Male elk grow to about eight hundred and fifty pounds. Females reach about six fifty," the ranger rambles on. "With our mild winters and plentiful vegetation, these Kentucky elk are already outweighing their western cousins. All that chomping is kind of a headache for the coal company, though, since the elk can be kind of rough on the grass and shrubs. You'll see what I mean here in a few minutes, if we're lucky and the herd is where I saw it yesterday."

Ranger Whit starts to put the microphone back in its stand, but thinks better of it. "Now, I know some of you out-of-state folks might not think too kindly about coal mining, but these elk are proof positive there's a lot of good that comes from it, too. Besides that, here in Kentucky, coal puts food on our tables—mine, for instance, when I was growing up."

JD snickers. "I wonder how much my old man pays him to say that."

My thoughts flash on Ma and little Zeb drowning in a river of sludge because of all that helpful coal, and then just as quick, a memory of fishing with my daddy on a mountain lake pops into my mind. I remember him showing me how to hold a rod and "tease a fish." I can still feel the warmth of his rugged hand over mine.

"Ranger Whit?" My voice cracks as I try to make myself heard over the whining of the bus's engine pulling us up the mountain. He looks up and nods at me through the oversized rearview mirror. "Is there a lake near here . . . where people fish?"

"Are you talking about Crystal Lake?" he asks.

"Maybe. There was a pier. They kept the lake well stocked." I remember the first fish I ever caught, a speckled trout that was too small to keep. Daddy made me throw it back and I cried.

"Yeah, that was a great place. It's just about a mile from here. Can't fish it anymore, though." Ranger Whit is pretty much yelling his answers back to me as the bus continues to grind its way up the hill. "Things kind of died off."

"How come?" We pass a gigantic coal truck parked on the side of the road—each tire the size of a car, its coal bed as deep as a swimming pool.

"Not sure." He shakes his head. "Could have had something to do with runoff from the local mine."

"Another benefit of coal?" I blurt out before I can catch myself.

Ranger Whit shrugs his shoulders up to his ears like it baffles him, too, and I feel bad for making that smart-alecky comment. I'm sure he's not any happier about the fate of that lake than I am. I'm starting to feel sorry for myself—I mean, even my good memories are becoming tainted by the likes of coal—when JD raises his fist.

"*Dude*. That was *awesome*."

I'm surprised by his praise, but I bump his fist anyway, which makes me feel kind of cool, maybe for the first time in my life. Even Jules is grinning like I passed some kind of test.

Eventually, the road levels out and a vast, lunar-like landscape opens up before us—solid, gray rock and hard-packed dirt as far as the eye can see. There are mountains in the distance, hinting green, but the stony wound in front of us is so wide and gaping that it looks like God Himself swiped away the mountaintop with one mighty claw—if He had one, that is, and I'm not saying He does.

Ranger Whit opens the bus's folding door and we all pile out, approximately twenty-five senior citizens, three scruffy kids, and a park ranger who's trying his best to see the good in everything.

"Over there." Ranger Whit points east, where a red sun is starting to cut through the rainy mist. I think maybe he's pointing at some elk, so I raise Papaw's binoculars up to my eyes and squint. No elk. Just a skyscraper-tall crane and a whole lot of rock.

"That's the active mining site," he explains. "See that contraption? That's what they call a dragline. It's the machine that digs into the rock to expose the coal. It weighs up to eight million pounds; it's twenty stories tall, and its base is as big as a gymnasium. Isn't that something?"

Jules tugs at my elbow. "Curley, are you okay? You don't look so good."

"Yeah, dude," JD adds, "you look like you've seen a ghost or something. Don't tell me you've never seen MTR before?"

At first I think he's talking in text, like OMG or LOL, but then I put it together. Mountaintop removal. "Sure, I've seen it." I shrug like it's no big deal. After all, I don't want him to think I've lost my "cool."

Truth is, the closest mountaintop removal site to Wonder Gap is the one with that faulty sludge pond a couple of mountains over from us, but I've never seen it up close. When I was a little guy, Mama told me there were monsters up there; she didn't want me going near it. Later, a couple years after she died, I hiked partway up, but only got as far as the company gate. I didn't have the stomach to cross the line.

JD pulls a camcorder out of his backpack and hands it to me. "Here, Curley, my man. It looks like you could use something to do."

Jules adds, "Yeah, Curley. Get some video for our project. I bet you'll be good at that." She touches JD on the arm as she's smiling at me. Now that the sun is shining, I guess their little spat has evaporated along with the rain.

JD has just finished showing me how to zoom in and out (we practice on the dragline) when Ranger Whit spins around and points. "There! Look!" Off in the distance against a hill, a bull elk and six lady elk are gingerly picking their way through a field of spindly trees and shrubs.

"Aren't they beautiful?" an older woman about the age of my Aunt Gertie whispers, like she's in church or something. Other folks are grabbing their binoculars or snapping pictures.

Jules is standing on her tiptoes, something she does when she's excited. "Curley! I think that's our elk!"

I can't imagine how that could be, but I say, "Gosh, Jules, I think you're right." Her use of the word *our* has me wishing we were back in our tree.

"See how the elk have shredded the bark off those saplings?" The ranger nods. "That's a reclamation site, where they've planted vegetation after removing the coal, but I guess the elk don't know it. They think those trees and bushes were planted just for them."

A man in a camouflage jacket counts the points on the bull's rack. "Man, that would look good over my fireplace!" His wife hits him on the shoulder.

"Well, you might be doing us a favor." Ranger Whit scans the herd through his binoculars. "Since these elk were introduced to eastern Kentucky, their numbers have exploded, as I already mentioned. Fish and Wildlife now allows about one thousand hunting permits a year, but some say that's not enough. Some locals think elk are a nuisance, invading their yards, eating up their gardens, and causing accidents on county roads." He lets the field glasses drop to his chest. "But I think they're beautiful. I never get tired of seeing them."

I'm filming now. In the viewfinder, I've got Ranger Whit in the foreground with the elk herd in the distance. For some reason, it's easier to stomach the torn-up landscape when I'm viewing it from behind the lens, where the scene is squared off and small.

"So where did these elk come from . . . originally, I mean?" I lean in so the microphone will pick up Ranger Whit's answer. I'm thinking I can get most of my research done while we're up here. I give a quick glance around for JD and Jules, but they're nowhere to be seen.

"Good question! These are actually mountain elk, and they come from several western states, such as Kansas and Montana. They were shipped to Kentucky in livestock vans much like you'd ship cattle."

"So you might say they were invited? Like out-of-town guests?"

"Very much so. The Department of Fish and Wildlife figured elk would be good for tourism and, of course, the hunting industry. If the success of these elk tours is any indication, I'd say they were right."

"But now we're hunting them down because they've become a nuisance, even though we invited them?" That comment would certainly earn another fist bump from JD, if only he were around to hear it. Where *are* those two, anyway?

The ranger fixes his gaze on the ground, stirring the dirt with his boots. The rest of the tour folks have scattered, some to get a closer look at the elk, some to get a closer look at the mining site.

"Well, we didn't anticipate how quickly they'd adjust, son. Before the Eastern elk became extinct, cougars and wolves were their natural predators, as well as humans. But these elk here have no predators except for us. That's why, when you need to control a population like this, hunting is so helpful."

"Unless you're an elk," I say under my breath. I can tell by the look on the ranger's face that he heard me.

"What's your name, young man?"

"Curley, sir." I gulp and stop recording. I figure I must be in trouble. Why else do adults ask for your name?

"Well, Curley. I think you have a future as an investigative reporter. This interview isn't going to wind up on CNN, is it?" He laughs.

"No, sir. It's for a school report. No one will pay it any mind, I'm sure."

Papaw's always saying that being polite is your best weapon, and it must be working, because Ranger Whit pats me on the back real gentle-like and turns to leave. Suddenly, I realize that the camera's been recording all this time, when I thought I'd pushed STOP.

"Ranger Whit?"

"Yes?"

"There's one thing I still don't understand." I start a slow pan from the mountaintop removal site to the field where the elk are grazing.

"Sure, son, what is it?"

"Well, if the word *reclamation* means to bring something back to its original condition, then where's the *top* of the mountain? I mean, it seems that what we have here is a field, which is real nice for the elk, like you said, but as far as I can tell, sir, the mountaintop is *gone*."

"Well now, aren't you a smart little cuss?" He slaps his knee with his wide-brimmed hat.

"Honest, sir, I don't mean to be. It's just that my papaw's always telling me to make sure I'm using the right words. He says words are an agreement you make with other people."

"That so?"

"Yes, sir. Seems to me the word *reclamation* is just plain wrong. Seems to me that if you're going to remove the top from a mountain, a better word would be *irrevocable*, because there's no getting it back." That happens to be this week's word, and I'm glad to have it in my holster, not that the ranger's looking too happy about it.

"Sure you're not a reporter?" Ranger Whit shakes his head and starts walking away. "I don't know how to answer you, Curley," he yells back over his shoulder. "Seems like you've already made up your mind."

I watch him get smaller and smaller in the viewfinder as he heads toward a cluster of old folks taking pictures with their phones. I record a few more seconds of the elk herd and the lunar landscape, then head back to the bus. I've seen enough. For sure, Ranger Whit has seen enough of me.

I expect the bus to be empty, but no, Jules and JD are all tangled up in our backseat. They don't even see me. I slump into a front seat and wait for the tour to end.

Now I'm the broody one. I brood about dead lakes, topless mountains, and some coal boss's son kissing my best friend. Every stinking one of them—*irrevocable*.

There's no turning back.

━━━━━━━━

Irrevocable—*adjective*

: incapable of being recalled or revoked; unchangeable; irreversible; unalterable; as, an irrevocable promise or decree; irrevocable fate

Jules tells me that JD plays "a mean electric guitar." He probably plays it for her up in his bedroom, like I used to serenade her with my harmonica right here on our front porch. I'd play the blues on hot summer nights after the sun sank behind the mountains and the fireflies came out. Believe me, I know it's not the same. The guitar is cool and the harmonica is not.

I'm not ashamed to admit it: I love wailing on old Gloria. I named her after a song I heard on one of Papaw's Van Morrison records. I love how she fits snug in the cup of my hands, how I can carry her wherever I go.

My Uncle Pete from up in Chicago gave her to me a few years after Pa died. He and my aunt were driving through Kentucky on their way to Florida for a vacation. He used to play harmonica for a rhythm and blues band at a neighborhood bar when he was younger, but he figured I needed it more than he did now.

"It will always show you how you feel, Curley," he said. "Just reach inside your heart, close your eyes, and blow."

He gave me a few pointers before he left, like how to play several notes at once and how to create vibrato—a kind of shimmery sound—but mostly, he said I'd be able to teach myself. It's that kind of instrument. "When people let you down, you can always count on your blues harp to listen," he said. "It will be your best friend."

Well, when I got back from the elk tour yesterday, I needed a friend real bad. I grabbed old Gloria and sat in a rocker out on the porch for what seemed like hours, wailing at the mountain. Papaw let me be until supper was ready, and even then he didn't grill me about what was wrong. Maybe he knew there was nothing he could say to make the situation with Jules any better.

JD's coming by in a few minutes with a laptop he's loaning me and to show me how to use this editing program for the video I took yesterday. Our project is due in a few weeks. When he called last night, he was all hog wild about the footage I took up on the mining site. He said Mr. A's going to go bonkers when he sees it, since everyone knows he hates Big Coal and anything that goes against the environment.

I figure JD was trying to make me feel better after yesterday's incident. Once the older folks started piling back onto the bus, both he and Jules yelled for me to come back and sit with them, but I just couldn't. I wound up jammed against a window, sharing the seat with an older couple about Papaw's age.

I'm still wailing at the mountain, blowing my blues through old Gloria, when JD and his dad pull up our driveway. Mr. Tiverton waves at me before turning the car around to leave. I guess JD will be walking over to the Cavanaughs' later to hang out with Jules. I'm pretty sure I'm not invited.

"Hey, Curley." JD raises his fist for another one of those bumps, but I let it hang in midair. "Nice sound, man."

"Hey." I stand up and slip the harmonica into my back pocket.

"Here." He hands me the laptop. "I found some cool stuff online. I downloaded a video on elk being relocated to Kentucky. I think you'll like it. Well, you won't *like* it, but I think you'll be able to use it." He seems downright twitchy.

Suddenly, I think about him having his arms around Jules in the back of the bus and I get mad all over again. Before I know what I'm saying, I blurt out, "So how's *Jules*?" There's a sickening tone to my voice, like how a first grader might sound, and I wish I could take it back.

"Well . . . uh . . . she's fine." He's staring down at the porch floorboards through his greasy bangs when suddenly his face lights up. "Oh, yeah . . . she's definitely *fine*."

"Fine" comes out all stretched out, like he's thinking about kissing her or worse, and he grins at me like I'm going to "ha-ha" him right back or punch him on the shoulder like those football jocks do when a pretty girl walks by. I don't really want to invite him in, but I need to know how to work the editing program, so I nod my head in the direction of the door. "Come on."

JD follows me into the kitchen, and we work at the table. He's already loaded the editing program on the computer, and we use the footage from the mining site for practice. In about an hour, I've pretty much got it down.

"You're not bad for someone who doesn't even own a computer," JD says as he shows me how to superimpose titles over video. His pointer fingers click, click, click across the keyboard, like chickens pecking seed. "If you get stuck, call me, okay? My social life is pretty nonexistent right now since we moved down here."

Except for Jules, I force myself not to say. "What about that video footage?"

"Oh, yeah. I almost forgot. I downloaded it this morning."

JD clicks on an icon, and up pops a video titled *Elk Restoration in Eastern Kentucky*. It starts out with a proud-looking hunter in an orange vest posing for the camera between the antlers of a fallen elk. The word *restoration* hovers over the hunter's gun, and I think of something Papaw told me this morning when he gave me my new word.

"Curley," he said, "some words will change the entire way you look at something. Take this week's word, *juxtapose*, for instance. It's a verb that simply means to put one thing next to another in order to compare the two, but whoa, Nelly. Sometimes that simple action will flip the shades up on something you were previously blind to seeing and this little explosion will go off inside your head. Boom!" And he smacked his palm against the table, making me jump.

So when JD starts the video, I notice how the word *restoration* is juxtaposed over that gun and then I look down at the body of that dead elk and then back up at the hunter's smiling face and, well, to tell you the truth, all that juxta-posing makes me mad. It's like they're saying, *Isn't this cool? We brought all these elk out here to Kentucky so we can kill them.*

Now, don't get me wrong, I like guns as much as the next guy. Papaw and I have a target set up in the field behind his woodshop, and I'm a pretty good shot. But ever since the age of ten, when I was out hunting with Papaw and one of his buddies brought down a doe, I haven't had the stomach for it. It wasn't the blood exactly, it was the breathing that got to me. And then watching the breathing stop.

The narrator's saying something about how the restoration of elk in eastern Kentucky has been a boon to both hunting and the tourist industry, when JD starts picking up where he left off about not having any friends.

"I guess that's the thing I miss most about Indiana, my brothers back in the 'hood."

I nod, even though I really don't know what it's like to have friends like that, except for Jules, of course. On the laptop, the video's narrator drones on and on as elk are corralled into a holding pen by men dressed in camouflage. They're poking them with sticks.

"My old man says he bought this company here in Hicksville to get me away from all of those bad influences back home—as if he isn't one of the worst. It's all about work to him. What's good for coal is good for us, he keeps saying, like it's one of those incantation thingies Jules and her mom talk about."

"Mantras?"

"Yeah, that's it. Like it's a friggin' mantra or something."

A big crowd of people—the narrator estimates three hundred—are all standing around this field waiting for the van doors to open. A bystander keeps saying how this is the best thing that's ever happened to Kentucky, when JD starts having a hissy fit right next to me.

"But you want to know the truth? I'll tell you the truth. James David Tiverton II couldn't care less about Mom or me. I mean it, Curley. I know you met him and I know how he can come across—like a good old boy, sympathetic to your cause and all—but I'm telling you: His heart is as black as coal."

JD's words stun me, like a wave of heat from a rip-roaring fire in our woodstove. I don't think I've ever witnessed so much hate, except for maybe in Carl Jenkins before he gave me that black eye. It's not just the hate, though. If what JD says about his father is true, Papaw and I are sunk. I stare at the video flashing across the screen. A cheer goes up from the crowd as elk come charging down the ramp and into the open field, some with collars on.

JD reaches across the table and taps STOP, freezing an elk midleap. "I'd have caught the first bus back to Indiana, Curley, if it weren't for you and Jules."

Well, I don't mind telling you, if JD's hate for his father had me plastered to my seat, this news has me shooting straight down through the floor.

"Me?" I say. I can believe Jules, but . . . *"Me?"*

He laughs. "Yeah. I know that sounds weird, but you're a lot like my friends back home." He fiddles with the silver piercing in his left eyebrow. "You say what you think."

"Uh . . . well . . . thanks . . . but . . . that's not exactly true." Like what I think about him, for instance.

JD presses SAVE and waits for the program to close. I'm relieved that our little tech session is ending, but then he says, "And then there's Jules—"

I let out a groan. I can't help it. I've been stuffing it since Jules set eyes on him.

"Jules says you guys have been best friends since forever."

My heart does this little flip. She talks about me?

"So I want you to know I'm not going to hurt her or anything. I know you're probably freaking out about that, me being an older guy and all." He forces a laugh. "You probably don't see a lot of nose rings or piercings back here in the hills, either."

I continue to stare at the freeze-frame of the leaping elk and don't say a word.

"Honest, man . . . me and Jules? We're just having some fun, you know?" He shrugs like he's shaking something off his shoulder. Like dandruff. For some reason, this little gesture hits me like a punch in the gut, when you'd think I'd be doing handsprings.

"Does she know that?" I say, sharper than I intend. I want to sound, well, lackadaisical. I want him to think that Jules and I have talked, that I know all about the "fun" they're having.

"Of course." He shrugs. "She's the one who keeps saying we shouldn't get too serious. Besides, I know I'm her first boyfriend and all and she's . . . well . . . sweet, you know? Spunky . . . but sweet. Not at all like the girls back home in Indiana." He spins his studded armband around on his wrist. "So no worries, Curley, my man. I'll take good care of her."

"Don't do me any favors." I slam the laptop shut and push my chair back from the table.

"Whoa—" JD puts his hands up in the air like he's surrendering to the cops. "Dude . . . I was just trying to ease your mind, you know, about our mutual interest. We're cool, right?"

"No, JD, we're *not* cool. First of all, Jules is more than a 'mutual interest.' She's my *friend*. Second, you talk about her like you know her, but you don't. You don't know the first thing about her. You don't know her *at all*." I'm working up steam to say a lot more, when Papaw sticks his head around the kitchen door.

"Everything all right in here, boys?"

"Yeah, Mr. Weaver." JD grabs his backpack. "I was just going."

Papaw meets my steely gaze with his own cold stare. "Curley? Don't you have something to say to JD here?" JD freezes in front of the door, waiting.

I know what Papaw is expecting me to say, how he wants me to thank JD for "everything," but how can I? Sometimes when you *juxtapose* things, it makes you feel sad or even mad because it shows you how wrong something is—like when I juxtapose JD and Jules. Sometimes that "new light" Papaw talks about being cast is more like a shadow, blotting out everything good.

I meet JD's eyes as he turns around expectantly.

"No, Papaw. Don't worry." I wave my hand in the air like I'm shooing away a fly. "I already said it."

———

Juxtapose—*verb*

   : to place in nearness or contiguity, or side by side, often for the purpose of comparison

For the last four days, Jules and I have been walking to and from the bus stop together, just like in the old days before JD. Usually, I tell Jules the word for the week or she'll ask and we'll try to use it at least once on the way to school or on the way home. But this week, for some reason, I can't bring myself to tell her what it is. It feels like a secret before the thing that makes it a secret has had a chance to happen. Crazy, huh?

All I know is that I've been *fixating* (two years ago, February) on this dream catcher key chain I made for her in third grade that's clipped to a buckle on her schoolbag. At the time, I thought it was a sissy thing for a boy to be making, so all the materials I picked out—pipe cleaner, feathers, and beads—were black. I had in mind a dream catcher for a ninja warrior, which at the time I wanted to be.

"If you don't want it, I'll take it," Jules said after art class that day.

"Sure, here," I said, and the gift was made. I told her it would protect her against evil spirits, a stupid childish fantasy that's obviously not working.

Spring is coming to the mountain in spurts. Today is chilly after a couple of days of spitting cold rain. Jules and I slog our way home along the creek bed, trying to avoid crushing the clusters of bloodroot blossoms poking out here and there, like tiny white asterisks among all the dead leaves. When I was a little boy, I used to get terrible sore throats. Ma would use bloodroot to make a powerful medicine, mixing the bitter, red juice of its roots with maple sugar to hide the taste, which it never quite did. She always looked so worried about me, though, so I kept the bad taste to myself.

"JD tells me your part of our elk project is really coming along." Jules's voice sounds like a little girl's as it breaks the silence between us.

Since the elk tour, Jules and I have managed to keep JD out of our conversations. It's as if we were both pretending he didn't exist, which suited me just fine, so I have to wonder why she's bringing him up now. I decide to take the high road.

"Yeah, he was a big help with the video I'm making." I say this matter-of-factly, like JD and I are buds, like I didn't almost kill him last Sunday afternoon.

"Oh? He told me he wasn't so sure. Something about you getting your underwear all bunched in a wad." She stops to shift her pack to the other shoulder and examines me, like she's trying to read my face and probably my mind, something she's usually pretty good at.

"Oh, really?" I notice the dream catcher swinging from its chain. "*He* was the one who got himself all in a tizzy talking about his old man taking him away from his 'brothers' up north, like he wishes he'd never come here." It doesn't feel good telling on anybody like this, even JD, but gosh darn it, he started it.

"He said that?" She looks at me as if she doesn't believe me, and that really ticks me off.

"Yeah . . . he even said he doesn't have a social life down here in Hicksville."

She flinches. It's barely perceptible, but I see it in her face above the place where her dimple usually shows up when she's smiling. *Good. What I said hurts.* But then this twinge of guilt starts pinching at me and I have to tell the whole truth, which, I don't mind telling you, I absolutely hate.

"Except for you," I say, rolling my eyes. I kick an old rotted log and it crumbles. Jules gets all shy and wispy, like a feral kitten in from the cold.

"Well, that's *nice*," she says.

I think about telling her that JD said they weren't serious, that they were just "having fun," but then I see how she's blushing again, and I don't have the heart. Will I ever see the day when she blushes at the thought of *me*?

"Hey, Curley, would you hold my bag? I've got to pee." She shoves her pack at me without waiting for an answer and tromps off into the woods behind a tree.

I look at the dream catcher, pretty ratty after all these years but still intact, and I wonder if she'd miss it. Well, I guess we'll just have to see. Without a second thought, I unclip it from the buckle and stash it in the front pocket of my jacket. I squelch the guilt that's rising in my throat like bile, telling myself that the dream catcher is mine anyway.

I made it.

I gave it.

And I can take it back.

Jules and I have been peeing in the woods since we were knee-high to grasshoppers, and there's always been an unspoken rule that the other one never looks. My recent theft has *emboldened* me (last year, August), and I sneak a peek. I don't see anything, not really. Just Jules zipping up her jeans as she comes from around the tree.

Now *I'm* blushing. I'm not sure if it's what I saw or what I did that has me embarrassed, but thankfully, Jules doesn't seem to notice.

"Thanks," she says as she takes her bag back. "Let's get home. I'm freezing."

We walk by the sycamore tree where we sat and watched our first elk. Since JD came to Wonder Gap, Jules hasn't wanted to climb up on Ol' Charley anymore and hang out with me.

"Do you think we'll ever see that bull elk again?" I ask, hoping to remind her of that time we dillydallied the morning away.

"Naw." She looks up toward the mountain where the elk bellowed his mating call. The new green leaves of spring blur the line of sight we had when the branches were bare. She resumes walking, as if nothing happened up there that day when time stood still. "My guess is that old bull has gone back to where he came from," she says.

If only a certain bad boy would do the same.

———————

Kleptomaniac—*noun*

: one who exhibits an irresistible propensity to steal

"I'm sick and tired of seeing you sitting around sick and tired, so I'm putting you to work," Papaw tells me as he nods toward his workbench.

When he hands me a piece of sandpaper and a box full of thin wooden sticks about an inch long, I groan. He uses the sticks to attach wheels to a toy wagon he makes for an Appalachian crafts store up in Berea. He pays me a nickel a stick, which, I don't mind saying, isn't enough. There's got to be a hundred of them.

I've been moping around the house all weekend, ever since I became a thief. Mainly I've been holed up in my room, staring at the top drawer of my dresser where I hid Jules's dream catcher, just in case she comes over. I pushed it into the way back, past a mess of baseball cards, old Bazooka gum wrappers, and about a dozen or so arrowheads Jules and I dug up from Ma's garden when we were kids. I'm so beside myself with guilt, I haven't even had the gumption to play old Gloria.

Papaw knows my brooding has something to do with Jules, but I refuse to tell him what. "There's no stuck feeling so stubborn that a good *metaphor* won't move," he says, and I wonder what the heck he's getting at.

"Is that my word, Papaw? *Metaphor*?"

I already know all about metaphors from this poet who came to visit us in grade school. Our teacher called him a writer in residence. We thought that meant he slept on a cot in the janitor's storage room. I remember he helped us come up with over a dozen metaphors for the word *love*. My favorite was "Love is a scraggly old cat that will never leave you." Jules thought of that.

"What's gotten into you, Curley, my boy? We're only on *l*." Papaw peers at me across the workbench, as if he's trying to read me, but I'm a closed book. *Now, there's a metaphor*, I think, feeling spiteful.

Papaw hands me a rag and a rusty can of wood stain for when I'm finished with the sanding. "You can have *metaphor* next week, if you like."

"Whatever." He hates it when I say that. "What's *metaphor*

got to do with our *l* word, anyway?" I'm not in the mood for guessing.

"Sometimes when an object is a perfect metaphor or symbol for something, the word for it takes on that metaphor permanently, as part of its meaning. This week's word is one of them."

"You're losing me, Papaw. Just tell me what it is, *okay*?" I'm slumped over the workbench, sanding this teeny-tiny piece of wood with a teeny-tiny piece of sandpaper, wishing that Papaw would forget all about his stupid words just this once.

"You're holding the word in your hand, Curley. A form of it, anyway."

I look down at the measly little stick I'm sanding and hold it up between my thumb and forefinger. *"This?"*

"Yup. It's called a *linchpin*. It's what holds the wheel on the wagon, right?"

"Uh . . . *yeeaaah* . . ."

"You know that thing I sometimes say when a plan falls apart? *The wheels just fell off?* Well, the name for 'a pin that locks a wheel into place' also means the key thing that holds something together, whether it's a plan, a project, or a relationship. You pull the linchpin, and the whole thing falls apart."

My mind flashes to Jules and JD, and I wonder what their linchpin is and what would happen if I pulled it. I think about telling Jules what JD said about not being serious, and in my mind's eye, I see JD running down a hill after a runaway wheel while Jules leaps from a wagon into my arms. The picture makes me smile.

I don't think this is what Papaw had in mind to get me out of my mood, but the metaphor is working nonetheless.

The next day in the lunch line, I ask Jules if I can stop by her house after school for some help on the narration I'm writing for the video.

"Sure, Curley. I've got something I want to tell you, anyway," she says, and I could swear I see her face pink up a bit as she grabs a tray from the wire rack. Could she and JD be breaking up? Has she come to her senses and realized that I'm the one for her? Maybe I won't have to pull that linchpin after all.

Jules and her ma live in a double-wide, one of the nicer ones in Wonder Gap. It's got flower boxes under all the windows, which Mrs. C keeps loaded up with red geraniums during growing time, and a back porch where Jules and I mountain watch, sipping sweet tea.

I might as well tell you, there's no *Mr.* C. I guess Jules's daddy up and left right after she was born; her ma was just seventeen. With the same dark, curly hair as her daughter, Mrs. C looks more like she's Jules's older sister than her ma. Even their voices sound alike. When they're chatting away in the car and I close my eyes, it's impossible to tell them apart.

Mrs. C has made a good life for herself and Jules, that much is for sure, tending her garden, raising chickens, and making everything from scratch. In addition to selling homemade soaps and lotions, she keeps the books for businesses up in Fraleysburg, something she can do from home. "A girl needs her mama close by," she says. "I'm blessed the good Lord has shown me the way."

Mrs. C is sliding a sheet of lavender sugar cookies out of the oven when Jules and I come barreling through the back door into the kitchen. Mrs. C grows and dries her own lavender, so the whole house smells as fresh and hopeful as a spring day. She hands me a plate of cookies while Jules grabs two mugs of steaming hot cocoa. When I see that we're heading for Jules's room at the end of the hallway, my heart starts pounding against my chest like it has fists.

We've been hanging out in each other's rooms since we were little, so it's not as if I expect to make out with her or anything. Neither Papaw nor Mrs. C has ever ordered us to keep the door open or even checked up on us, except to tell one or the other it's time to go home. "It's like you're siblings, only better," Mrs. C said once. "You're not fighting for a parent's attention."

She was right, of course. The only attention I ever really wanted was from Jules. Today, though, I guess I'm hoping for a different kind.

Jules sets her mug down on her bedside table and hands me mine.

"Okay, Curley," she says as she plops herself down on the bed. "Show me what you've got."

I know she means the project, right? But my ears hear it differently. My face flares hot, which only embarrasses me more, which just makes the blood rush into my cheeks. I sit on the edge of the bed, holding the mug in one hand and balancing the plate of cookies on my lap with the other.

"Sure," I say. "In a minute . . . um . . . I need a cookie first, okay?"

106

"Sure." She grabs one, too, and the plate wobbles a bit. I set my mug on it to hold it steady.

Usually, Jules would be the one jabbering on and on about stuff, but today, the only sound in the room is an occasional nibble or slurp. I've heard Jules mimic JD witnessing an uncomfortable situation like this at school, chanting, "Awkward . . . ," but thankfully, she doesn't say that.

"Curley, I've got something to tell you, and it can't wait." She's winding and rewinding a clump of hair around her finger. "I still can't believe this happened." She looks upset, and I wonder what he did to her. If he hurt her, I'll kill him. "I didn't want to tell you until I was sure . . ."

Sure of what? My love? Her love? His lies?

". . . that I lost it."

Oh. *That.*

"Lost what?" I ask, hoping to look clueless.

"Lost your dream catcher, that's what." She's acting like it's all her fault. "You know, the one you made me that I've had all these years?"

Technically, I didn't make it for her; she took it, but I figure this isn't the time to bring that up. Besides, I'm the one who stole it back, and I'm not feeling real good about that right now. There are tears in her eyes.

"I feel so bad, Curley. I don't know how I could have been so careless. It must have fallen off my book bag somehow, but the truth is, I don't even know how many days it's been gone."

"Oh, Jules . . . that's okay. It's bound to turn up sooner or later, you'll see." I'm already plotting how to sneak it into her locker without her seeing me.

"But I've looked everywhere for it."

I look around her room and notice for the first time clothes piled helter-skelter on the floor, her two orange beanbag chairs stacked in the middle of the room, her dresser pulled away from the wall.

"Golly, Jules, it *does* look like a cyclone blew through here big-time." I set the empty cookie plate and mug on her desk, then come back and sit cross-legged on the bed, facing her. Maybe if I make light of it, she'll calm down, but then I take one look at her face and see another storm brewing.

"You don't understand!" Her face is all contorted, and I wonder if she's found me out, but instead she says, "I've been such a *terrible* friend." And then she drops her head into her hands and sobs.

"Jules?"

I can't even begin to tell you how much I hate seeing her this way, knowing I'm the cause of it. I'm about to bust out with the truth, when she looks up at me. Her tears must be acting like prisms, because I swear I've never seen her eyes so bright.

"Jules?" I reach out and she falls into my arms, crying even harder. "You're *not* a terrible friend," I say as I pat her back gently. My fingers tangle in her hair.

"Am, too, Curley. Ever since JD got here, I've been ignoring you." She talks into my shoulder, and I can feel the wetness of her tears soaking through my shirt.

"When I lost that dream catcher, it made me realize how I've taken you for granted, how you've always been there for me, but how lately, I haven't been there for you. How can you even *stand* me?"

I'm grappling for an answer, when I realize it's one of those questions girls ask that you're supposed to ignore. One side of my face is smooshed up against her hair and it's tickling my nose, but the way she feels in my arms . . . *well*, I'm thinking maybe being a kleptomaniac isn't such a bad thing, when she pulls back out of my arms and is glaring at me again.

"I'm also really *mad* at you for not being nicer to JD. He's lonely, you know, and you've been really childish. I mean, just because I have a boyfriend doesn't mean you and I stop being friends, or that you stop being *you*. I know you, Curley. You're kinder than that."

One thing I both love and hate about Jules is how she can cut through the excrement and get right to the truth, which, I don't mind saying, usually hurts. Thing is, I don't know which hurts worse—her calling JD her boyfriend or calling me less than kind. I'm wishing for the guilty Jules over the honest one, when she reaches for my hand.

"Never mind all that. What I'm trying to say, Curley, is that I've been a terrible friend and I'm sorry. I don't want to lose you. One thing we've always been able to count on is our honesty with each other. Nothing . . . and no one . . . is as important to me as that."

The truth about the dream catcher is burning inside me. She squeezes my hand, and I think I'll explode. Telling her about what JD said is no longer the point. It's *my* truth that counts here. The truth about *me*.

I'm about to 'fess up, when she raises her pinky in the air, an invitation to interlock with mine. It's the way we end all our fights.

"Friends?" she asks.

I hesitate. What if the truth is the linchpin that makes all of this fall apart? How can I risk that? How can I not? I sigh. Her eyebrows furrow, no doubt wondering if I'm having second thoughts. And then her dimple shows.

Call me a coward, but I just can't disappoint her. Not now.

I raise my pinky and link it with hers.

"Friends," I say.

When I get home, Papaw's in the living room sitting in the dark. The shades are drawn, and he doesn't even have a fire going in the woodstove. His dark green flannel shirt blends into his easy chair's corduroy slipcover. The only thing that seems to add light to the room is his mane of silver hair.

I usually don't bother him if he's napping, but the heaviness in the room scares me. It reminds me of the wake the Donnelly sisters held for my ma and little Zeb when Papaw said he couldn't do it.

"Papaw?"

He startles in his chair, as if from a dream. "Curley? You home already?"

"Yeah, Papaw. Are you okay?"

When he doesn't answer right away, I remember that he was supposed to have a meeting with Mr. Tiverton today. How could I forget? Too busy feeling guilty over Jules's dream catcher to remember that the fate of my life with Papaw is hanging by a thread, that's how. Folks say they see red when they're angry, but all the red I'm seeing is on account of shame.

"Papaw, what happened?" I let myself fall back onto the couch in front of him. I pull the silver chain of the brass lamp on my right and gaze into his face, trying to read what's there. Even in the warmth of the light, his skin looks gray. His eyes are without their usual shine. I swallow hard. "Do we still have a deal?"

"Yeah, Curley. There's a deal on the table, anyway."

"Then what's wrong?"

He leans forward, elbows on knees, staring down at the rag rug under his feet. He shakes his head and hair falls over his eyes.

"I'm having a hard time finding the stomach to accept it."

Speaking of stomachs, mine does this sinking tumble, like what it did in the elevator of the Willis Tower last summer when we visited my Uncle Pete in Chicago. Papaw raises a hand, signaling me to wait with my questions, which is just as well, because all of my questions are in the pit of my gut.

"I told him I'd have to think about it, that I wanted to talk to you first. He said he'd give us a month before he moves on anything."

"Moves on what, Papaw?"

"Moves on our mountain, Curley."

"Our *what*?" His words aren't making sense until my mind flashes on the topless mountain on Ranger Whit's elk tour. "He's *not* . . ."

"I'm afraid he is." Papaw looks up and latches on to my gaze. "We either agree to stand by, take our money, and say nothing. Or we say something and lose everything . . . *including* our mountain."

"What kind of choice is *that*?"

"*Exactly*. I keep rackin' my brain, searching for an answer, but no answer comes. It's a conundrum, Curley . . . which is why we're going to sit on it for a while. It's time to take stock."

I'm thinking it's time to blow up somebody's house. "But, Papaw. We can't lose our mountain." Tears are burning their way down my cheeks. "It's not fair!"

"*Fair* has nothing to do with it." Papaw reaches for the little bottle of heart pills by his chair and puts one under his tongue. "Technically, Curley, it's not our mountain. The government owns most of it, and Tiverton holds the lease on it. The land is his to do with as he pleases."

"But it *is* our mountain, Papaw. It's the one we look at every day. We have a right to it, too." I know Papaw isn't the enemy here, but my mad has nowhere else to go. "We can't stand by and watch it happen, Papaw." I rub the wet off my cheeks with my sleeve, feeling the strength of a resolve I didn't know was in me. "We just *can't*."

———

Linchpin—*noun*

1 : a pin used to prevent the wheel of a vehicle from sliding off the axletree

2 : that which holds a thing together and without which, a thing falls apart

M

I should be paying attention.

Carl Jenkins and one of his cronies are in the middle of their report on the extinction of the Carolina parakeet—something about their feathers being used in ladies' hats, blah, blah, blah, blah, blah. If I'm not careful, Mr. A's yardstick is going to land smack across the lab table in front of me. Not that I care. As a matter of fact, let it. I'll just grab that stick and smack him right back with it, I'm so steamin' mad.

I'm mad at Mr. A for not being a better friend to Papaw. I'm mad at Papaw for taking so long to decide what to do about our mountain. I'm mad at JD for the usual reasons and at Jules for being so hoity-toity honest and good. But most of all, I'm mad at myself for sitting around stewin' when I should be doing something, anything, to stop Tiverton Coal from blowing up our mountain. Not that I have the slightest idea *what*.

Jules is sitting so close to me that the sleeve of her sweater keeps brushing against my arm. I wish she'd go ahead and cuddle up with JD, who's sharing our lab table with us. The poster collage of elk they worked on together lies facedown in front of them. I think about all the time they spent on it, cutting and pasting, and I want to tear it apart.

Carl Jenkins grabs Mr. A's yardstick to use as a pointer. A gutsy thing to do, I'll give him that. He points to an easel on top of Mr. A's desk with a blown-up picture of a Carolina parakeet—all bluish green with an orange-red head, like something you'd find in Florida. *No wonder everybody wanted their feathers,* I think, which makes me mad all over again. Why does everyone always want to destroy what's pretty to look at? Like mountains, for instance.

"Any questions for our presenters?" Mr. A scans the room with his laser-like eyes, and I try not to meet his gaze. Too late. "Mr. Hines? You look lost in thought. Care to share?"

"I do *not*." Those three little words come out sharp as nails, and everyone stares.

"Oh, come on, Curley . . . please *share*." This from Carl Jenkins in a syrupy voice filled with its usual venom.

Thwack. Carl hits his parakeet poster with Mr. A's yardstick, I guess to assert some kind of power over me, but it rocks the easel until it teeters and falls right into Mr. A's trash can. Naturally, the whole class erupts into uncontrollable laughter, and I'm off the hook. At least I think I am until Mr. A quietly pulls the easel out of the trash can and addresses me again.

"Well, Mr. Hines. Let's hope Mr. Jenkins pays you the same kind of rapt attention during your presentation you've paid him. You and your buddies are up."

Jules and JD push back their chairs at the same time and grab the poster. Their part of the presentation comes first. Jules insisted on practicing their spiel in front of me over the weekend, taking both parts since JD was in Indiana visiting his mom. Every time I was about to tell her about Mr. Tiverton's "offer," she'd say, "Wait a minute, Curley. I need to change something," and scribble on one of her note cards. Finally, when I was getting ready to go home, she asked, "What's up?" but I decided not to tell her just for spite. As I watch the two of them position the poster collage on the easel, I want to be anywhere else but here.

Their voices drone on, a duet about Eastern elk I already know by heart. I should be listening for my cue, but my mind keeps flipping back to Papaw slumped in his chair, not knowing what to do. If someone as smart as Papaw doesn't have the answer, then what could a no-account twelve-year-old boy from Wonder Gap, Kentucky, possibly do to stop the likes of a powerful coal boss from blowing the top off a mountain?

"Curley?" Jules's voice breaks through a cloud of whispers. "Come *on*." She motions for me to get up. "It's your turn." JD is busy hooking up his laptop to the TV sitting on a cart in front of the whiteboard.

"Mr. Hines?" Mr. Amons calls from across the room. "Today would be good."

I grab my notes from the back of my science textbook and push by Jules to get to the front of the room. JD hands me the controller and says, "Go get 'em, Ketchup," a name he calls me on account of Hines being a brand name for condiments even though it's not spelled the same. His calling me that ticks me off so much, the stack of notes in my left hand rattles. I set them down on Mr. A's desk.

I point the controller at the laptop and punch the START arrow. The image of the hunter grinning over his dead elk pops onto the screen.

"Oh, man, look at that rack!" Carl blurts out. "That's gotta be an eight pointer!"

"Well, what do you know?" JD smirks. "Jenkins can count!"

Carl lunges from his seat.

Thwack! Mr. A has his yardstick back. Meanwhile, I've hit PAUSE.

"Gentlemen. That's enough!" Mr. A points the stick at Carl, who slowly lowers himself back into his chair, staring daggers at JD. "Proceed, Mr. Hines."

I press PLAY again and the title from the original video appears on the screen, which I try to read aloud. Here's how it comes out: "Th Relothcathen of Elth in Ethern Kenthucthy." My throat is so dry, my tongue is sticking to the roof of my mouth like flypaper.

"Speak up, Mr. Hines," Mr. A yells from the back of the room, where he's sitting at a lab table with Anna Ludlow. "Here, try this." Over the heads of my classmates, he throws me a mini water bottle, which, fortunately, I catch in midair. "You need some spit."

I chug about half the bottle. As I swallow, my Adam's apple feels gigantic, which is something I'm already self-conscious about. Meanwhile, the room is dead quiet, which does little to set me at ease. Darn Mr. A, anyway. I had wanted to add the narration to the video, so I wouldn't have to go through this, but he insisted I deliver my part of the presentation in person.

"I want to hear the resonance of your persuasive voice," he'd said, which I thought sounded like a crock of excrement, but I held my tongue, which goes to show: I'm learning.

"Okay," I say, pressing PLAY one more time. "Let's try this again." A big green X slashes across the first title on the screen, and the second title—the one I wrote—appears in bold red script. I told Papaw I thought it was a tad overdramatic, but he'd said, "Sell it," so I do. "You can never go wrong with a *metaphor*," he'd said, which is this week's word, of course.

"Elk: Pawns in a Deadly Game of Chess," I read. This time, my words come out sounding clear and sharp. "It had been over a hundred years since anyone saw an elk in eastern Kentucky, since before the Civil War." I take another sip of water to keep my tongue good and wet. "As my partners pointed out, the Eastern elk were long gone—make that *extinct*—after being over-hunted, probably by folks much like this guy here.

"So in 1997, a group of people got an idea." An artist's etching of an Eastern elk slowly fades onto the screen. "Never mind the Eastern elk. Never mind their unique size and beauty. Never mind that they're gone forever. We'll just take another kind of elk, some mountain elk from out west, and transplant them here in Appalachia."

At this point in the video, I've created a simple animation of an elk being picked up by a cartoon hand and moved across a map drawn to look like a chessboard. I had to call JD to ask him how to do all that, so I guess I owe him one, which I'm not real happy about. The elk has a fake smile on its face.

"No one will ever know the difference, right?" I pause and look at my audience. The elk's smile turns into a frown. "Except, of course, the elk." Most of the class laughs at this, and I've got to tell you, I'm feeling pretty good.

As I continue my narration, the video goes on to show those first elk being rounded up in Kansas and loaded onto a cattle truck by a bunch of guys dressed in camouflage.

"This is some of the scenery the elk might have seen if they'd been given windows," I say as the video shows clips of the elk's thousand-mile trek cross-country. That whole section ends in the hills of Kentucky, of course, with the elk rushing down a ramp, scattering every which way like they're looking for something.

"Guess they're wondering where home went," I add, a comment not in my notes. Out of the corner of my eye, I see Mr. A cover his mouth, muffling a laugh.

"The elk have settled in real nice, however," I continue. Now we're seeing the footage I took up on the mountaintop removal site. "Their numbers have exceeded expectations."

I go on to give some statistics about elk reproduction and how people are now finding them a nuisance. Considering how nervous I was initially, I can hardly believe how relaxed I'm feeling. I give a quick glance toward Jules and she's beaming. As JD would say, I'm on a roll.

That is, until I look at the footage of what used to be a mountain and I lose my train of thought. I look down at my notes for the first time, but the words are a blur. All I can think about is *my* mountain and how Mr. Tiverton wants to blow it up. I look up at the TV and see the beginning of the long, slow pan I took of the mining site, and my eyes begin to burn.

A few kids fidget in their seats. Carl and his buddies are snickering, and Jules is giving me her bug-eyed, "get with it" look. JD's brooding eyes are riveted on my face, as they have been from the beginning, but I can't tell whether he's sending me good luck or a curse.

I toss my notes in the trash.

"Who cares?" I mumble.

"What's that, Mr. Hines?" Mr. A stands up and shouts from the back of the room. "I can't hear you."

"Who cares?" I shout back.

Heads turn from Mr. A to me.

"Who cares that the Eastern elk are now extinct?" I shout, stabbing the PAUSE button on the remote. The frame freezes on a far-off elk herd against a backdrop of blasted stone.

"Who cares if a species goes extinct? There are plenty other kinds, right? Like these mountain elk from Kansas and Colorado. We'll just get us some of those." I rewind the video and begin the slow pan of the mining site all over again.

"Who cares where they came from when they look so pretty in our mountains, right?" I freeze the picture on the dragline, that twenty-story monster that sits smack-dab in the middle of that gosh-awful lunar landscape. "But wait . . . Where's the mountain?" I press PLAY and the pan continues. "I could have sworn there was a mountain here a year ago. Where did it go?"

I let the pan run out until it fades to black.

"Oh, well. Who cares? Who cares that the mountaintop is

gone? Who cares that the Eastern elk are gone? Who cares that the Carolina parakeet is gone? Who. Cares. That. We. Will. Never. Get. Any. Of. Them. Back. Ever. Who cares?"

I shrug and scan the room. Many of my classmates are staring back at me as if I've fallen completely off my rocker. At least, that's what I believe until Anna Ludlow raises her hand. I think she has a question. Her voice is small. I feel it more than hear it.

"I care," she says.

JD raises his hand, slowly, deliberately, like a flag drawn to full mast.

"I care," he says.

Pretty soon, there's another hand in the air . . . and then another . . . and another. Within seconds, the whole room is ringing with the most astonishing chorus of words I've ever heard.

"I care."

"I care."

"I care."

Of course, Carl Jenkins is still staring hate daggers at me. The fact that his cronies have dared to say "I care" probably has something to do with it. Jules also has been staring at me with a look I can't quite decipher. She seems stern or darkly thoughtful. Like I said, I'm not sure.

Finally, after everyone has taken their turn, Jules raises her hand. It's as if she's been waiting to have the last word, something she's good at, incidentally. She keeps her hand in the air, waiting for me to acknowledge her, like I'm the teacher or something, so I nod.

"I care, Curley Hines," she says. "Do you?"

I wait until the entire room goes silent. I don't know why. I guess I want to make sure there's a place for my words to land.

"Yes, ma'am." I return her gaze. "I do."

"Ooooh . . . it's like they just got married!" Carl squeals like a stuck pig.

I guess he thinks he can ruin the moment, but in a way, he helps break the ice. Everyone laughs, including me and Jules, even JD.

Mr. A says we don't have time for another presentation, so he breaks out his entire bowl of chocolate candy. While everyone is still chattering and licking their fingers, he calls me up to his desk.

"Mr. Hines, I think you found your gift today."

"What's that, Mr. A?" I'm still thinking about Jules and the way she looked at me when I said, "I do."

"I mean that documentary you put together there and the way you talked to us. You made us *listen*, Curley. You made us *care*. I'm not sure anyone can teach you how to do that. It's as if you were born knowing how."

"Gosh, Mr. A, thanks . . . but I had help. Jules and JD, especially JD, helped a lot."

"That's awfully good of you, Mr. Hines, to give credit where credit is due." Mr. A waves his hand in the air like he's reconsidered everything he just said and is shooing me away. "I only wanted you to know that I think you've got something. Don't waste it."

I'm on my way back to our lab table when I notice Jules looking past me, quizzically, toward the classroom door.

"Mom?" she says.

I turn, and instead of Mrs. Cavanaugh answering her daughter, she looks straight at me. Her face is sad and pleading, but what could she want? I'm halfway to the door when my heart freezes and I don't want to know.

"Curley," she says. "It's Papaw."

Metaphor—*noun*

: a word or phrase used in conjunction with another word or phrase, suggesting that what they represent is the same or similar, as in "Papaw is my mountain."

Nobody wants me to go. They say there's nothing I can do to help, but I think it's just a lame excuse for keeping me in the dark. Even Jules fakes this cheerful "it's going to be all right" look on her face every time we talk about him. She insisted on giving me this week's word, because "Papaw wouldn't want me to miss one." A word I'm finding entirely useless, by the way.

I haven't been able to sleep a wink or eat much, not even Mrs. C's cheesy grits, since she came to school last Monday to tell me about Papaw's heart attack and then take me in. I had other offers—from Mr. A and even JD's dad—but I wanted to stay close to home, and shacking up with the enemy was out of the question.

Aunt Gertie calls me every day from the hospital and tells me Papaw's stable, but I'm pretty sure she's lying along with everyone else. *Poor Curley*, they're all thinking. *Lost his pa and then his ma and brother, too. Now this.* They're all in cahoots, as Papaw would say, and not one of them has the guts to tell me the truth.

None of them except Mr. A. He's all about finding out the facts. "Verify, verify, verify," he's always saying, which is why he's driving me up to Lexington so we can both see for ourselves. The chocolate milk shake he got me from McDonald's on our way out of Fraleysburg tasted pretty good—the first thing I've been able to stomach all week—but now my gut's back in a tangle.

"Now, Curley . . . your papaw's not going to look so good," Mr. A warns me as we speed-walk through the atrium of the hospital on the way to the cardiac care unit. He's got a death grip on my shoulder and he's steering me like a plow. I'm glad for this, never having been to a hospital before.

"Triple bypass surgery," I say offhandedly, like I've got it together. "Aunt Gertie told me all about it."

"Right."

Mr. A's face looks all shadowy gray. I wonder if he remembered to shave.

Minutes later, we're standing in front of Room 322. On a slip of paper in a slot under the number, *John Weaver* is penciled in.

"This is it." Mr. A leans on the handle, and the door heaves open.

I brace myself, but we find ourselves standing in a small entryway in front of a sink. I sneak a look through a rectangle of glass on the second door but only see the blur of a body, probably my aunt, sitting in a blue chair at the foot of a hospital bed. A sign over the sink says, WASH HANDS BEFORE ENTERING.

I thought there wasn't anyone in the world I wanted to see more than Papaw right now, but here I am rubbing my hands raw with an antiseptic soap that smells like the opposite of life itself. Suddenly, I'm not so anxious to verify the facts.

Mr. A and I toss our paper towels into a stainless steel bin. He looks down at me and smiles. "Ready?" I nod, even though I'm not.

My aunt stands and gives me a hug, but all I can look at is this old man tucked in tight like a mummy, faceup, in bed. His eyes are closed. His face is pale and unshaven. Tubes go in and out of his arms. Plastic bags on metal stands drip, drip, drip. Monitors blink and beep.

That's my papaw. I know it. And I want to touch him. But I can't. Those tubes are everywhere. His skin hangs loose around his neck. It's so thin that I can see a network of veins like branches of tiny trees streaming across his chest. Blue like mountains.

I'm afraid to touch him. I'm afraid my fingers might poke right through his skin.

A hint of roses, Aunt Gertie leans into me. "I'll leave the room so you can visit," she whispers and then disappears. Mr. A goes with her. And I am alone . . . with *him*.

I'm afraid to talk out loud, so I think to myself: *Papaw? Are you in there?*

His eyes pop open, and his whole body jumps like he's leapt right out of a dream.

"Curley?" His voice is soft and raspy, but it still sounds like him.

"Yup, it's me, Papaw." I bend over slightly so he can see me. "How are you feeling?"

"Like an elephant used my chest for a trampoline." His arms hug a heart-shaped pillow that lies across his chest. "This is for when I have to cough, or, heaven forbid, laugh," he says. "It helps hold everything together in there . . . you know . . . from the surgery."

"Oh."

The thought of what went on inside Papaw's chest takes the bones right out of me.

"Hey!" Papaw says, snatching my hand up with a familiar fierceness. "What the heck are you doing here, anyway?" It's like his touch sends this bolt of energy straight through me.

"Thought I'd check up on you, Papaw. Mr. A brought me up. We figured we needed to verify your whereabouts."

"Ha! You mean you needed to make sure I wasn't *dead*." He starts to laugh, but it quickly turns into a cough that makes his face twist up in what must be a heap of pain.

"Nurse!" I shout, desperately searching for some kind of emergency button. I'm here five minutes and I've already caused him to relapse or whatever it is people do when they take a turn for the worse.

"Curley," Papaw gasps, waving his hand in the air. "Never mind, son. Just hand me that cup of water, would you?" He nods toward the table at the side of his bed. I notice he's hugging his heart pillow real tight.

The cup has a bent straw in it. I hold it up to Papaw's mouth so he can drink. It feels good to be helpful, as opposed to . . . well . . . *detrimental* (d word, last July). Papaw pushes the straw away with his tongue and wipes his mouth with the edge of the hospital blanket. He takes a long breath in and lets it out nice and slow.

132

"Where is that good-for-nothin' old coot, anyway?" I know he means Mr. A. It's how he talks about him, especially after their falling-out.

"He stepped out with Aunt Gertie, Papaw, to give me some time alone with you."

"Uh-oh. That's bound to lead to no good."

A picture of Mr. A and my aunt making out in a dark corner of the hospital cafeteria pops into my head. "Eeeew, gross, Papaw, you can't mean—"

"Curley, he could be on his deathbed, and that rascal would still be chasing the ladies." The word *deathbed* crashes right through me, leaving terror in its wake. Papaw must sense it and quickly adds, "Look, Curley, I may be a little weak, but I'm on the mend. I won't be dying any time soon."

Tears stream down my cheeks, as hard as I try to hold them back. I feel like I'm three years old and losing my father all over again. "Really, Papaw?" My voice comes out all squeaky. As much as I want to believe what he says is true, my fear of becoming an orphan is even stronger. This is the fear that's been gnawing at me all week like a dog gnaws at a bone.

"Really. You and me, we're stuck with each other." He grips my forearm at the elbow and holds it firmly against his. In spite of all the tubes taped to his wrist, his touch makes me feel solid again. "The good Lord ain't done with me yet."

Papaw and I are linked up like that for a while, not talking, when I start to think about our mountain and what we're going to do. I know I shouldn't bother him with it. In fact, worrying about it is probably what landed Papaw in the hospital in the first place. But the month that Tiverton gave us is almost up, and we're still without a plan. I'm about to say something, when we hear the outer door click open and water running.

"Well, if it ain't John 'the Baptist' Weaver, alive and kicking!" Mr. A's booming voice precedes him into the room. I half expect to see him slapping his yardstick against the metal rails of Papaw's hospital bed. "I see St. Peter threw you back . . . or was that the devil who didn't want you?"

"Now, Percy." My aunt is about a foot shorter than Mr. A, so she tilts her head up to smile at him. She tucks a wisp of red hair behind her ear in a flirty sort of way. "I told you not to make him laugh," she says.

"No chance of that," Papaw whispers, but his words come out all tight. That's when I remember Mr. A is his mortal enemy and I'm the one who brought him here.

The smile on Mr. A's face drops into a frown. "Oh, come on, John," he says softly. "Let's let bygones be bygones. No use stirring up old muck. Not now."

The room gets real quiet.

Papaw looks at me and then over at his onetime friend and shrugs. I'm trying to determine if it's a "get lost" shrug or a "what the heck" shrug, when Aunt Gertie tugs at the sleeve of my jacket.

"Come on, Curley. Let's leave these boys alone." As she steers me from the room, I turn to see Mr. A stepping closer to Papaw's bedside.

I hope to heck it's safe.

Aunt Gertie and I go down to the hospital's cafeteria for a snack, but most of my fries turn cold and soggy on the plate, what with all the worry-thoughts churning in my gut. What if Papaw and Mr. A are at each other's throats? What if Papaw can't take care of me anymore? He says the good Lord ain't done with him yet, but what if He is? And what about our mountain? What if Tiverton Coal blows it up? What then? I need to know what Papaw wants us to do. We need a plan.

I guess Aunt Gertie can see that I'm anxious, so we don't stay away long. As we approach Papaw's room at the end of the hall, we can hear Mr. A's thunderous laughter rumbling through both steel doors.

"Your papaw's practicing how to laugh on the inside," Mr. A says defensively, predicting my aunt's protests as soon as we walk into the room. "It takes deep concentration, but I do believe he's getting the hang of it."

I check to see how tight Papaw's holding his heart pillow, when I notice he's wiggling his index finger up and down and grinning like a fool.

"That little motion there indicates how hard he's laughing." Mr. A leans back in the hospital chair and props a foot up on the bed railing. "Ingenious, don't you think?"

"Oh, yeah, your IQ is off the charts . . . but I won't say in what direction!" Aunt Gertie laughs. "For now, I think it's time for you and Curley to head for home." She pushes Mr. A's foot off the rail and reaches for his hand. "Come on, Percy. Let's let Curley say good-bye to his grandfather in peace."

When Papaw thanks Mr. A for bringing me up to see him, they both get to looking all misty-eyed. I think maybe Mr. A's going to bend over and kiss Papaw on the forehead—which would really be something to see—but then Papaw brushes him away and says, "Go on. Get out of here." Honestly, I think they're both so happy to be friends again they can hardly stand to look at each other.

As Aunt Gertie and Mr. A leave, a nurse comes in to take Papaw's blood pressure. She also gives him a pain shot, so I know we don't have much time before it takes effect. As soon as she's out the door, the question busts out of me.

"What are we going to do about our mountain, Papaw?"

Papaw sighs and leans back into his pillow. "As you can probably tell, Curley, I'm in no position to fight." I swallow hard. I was afraid he'd say that. "That doesn't mean you can't."

"Can't what?"

"Fight."

"Fight?"

"Yeah, fight. It doesn't mean you'll win, but it matters that you try."

"But how, Papaw? What can I do?"

A twelve-year-old fighting Big Coal? That painkiller must be dimming his brain. He closes his eyes like he's thinking, but he's quiet for so long, I think maybe he's fallen asleep. I'm about to tap him on the shoulder, when he starts talking again.

"When you were a little tyke, you'd get all frustrated over something that wasn't working out your way. You'd start kicking and screaming and your ma would finally say, real gentle-like, 'Curley, use your words.' And by golly, your words usually got you what you wanted." He opens his eyes and stares straight into mine with those steely blues. "That's how you fight, dear boy. I've given you a wagonload of words. Use them."

"Papaw, Mr. Tiverton said if we talked against coal, we'd lose our money. How are we going to live?"

Papaw's breathing slows way down, and I think maybe I've lost him—not in a dead-and-gone kind of way, but to sleep. I pull up so close to his ear I can see this tiny tuft of white hair sticking out of his earlobe in the place where the ear starts to curl.

"Papaw," I say again. "How are we going to live?" I'm about to give up and leave, when I hear him take a deep breath.

"I don't know," he says. And that's it.

That's the last thing Papaw says to me that day, not even good-bye.

———

On the ride home, I get a *niggle*.

That's what Jules would call it, anyway. It's the word she gave me this week, since Papaw couldn't. She says a *niggle* is an idea that comes to you by way of intuition—an inner kind of knowing you can't learn in books. Niggles often come out of the blue, she says. And sometimes they don't make sense. Like the one I just got.

"Stay with JD," this niggle says to me.

I say, *Huh?* Not out loud, of course. Mr. A would think I'm nuts. He's lost in his own world, anyway. So I begin to have this little conversation with myself, or maybe it's with the niggle. It goes something like this:

You've got to be absolutely out of your mind! Stay with JD?! He's the enemy . . . or at least the son of the enemy. A mortal enemy, if there ever was one.

"Stay with JD," the niggle says again.

Jules warned me about this. Rarely does a niggle explain itself, she said. I thought she was crazy. Now I know . . . *I* am.

But what will I do there? I'll have to eat with them, maybe even sleep in the same room with JD himself. What good could that possibly do?

"Stay with JD."

A niggle keeps on coming at you, apparently, kind of like a rabid hound, and it won't let you go until you've really heard it. None of this is in the Big Book, incidentally. This is straight from Jules.

Okay, let's say I stay with JD. Let's say I stay for a weekend. Will that be enough?

Silence.

Is that a yes?

Silence.

I don't believe this is happening.

———————————

Niggle—*noun*

According to Jules: an idea that bugs you until you listen to it

I call JD from Jules's house as soon as I get back. When I ask him if I can spend the following weekend with him and his dad, you'd think I told him he won the Kentucky Powerball Lottery.

"That's so cool, dude! We'll play pool and listen to music and then I'll teach you how to play *Battle King*. After my dad goes to bed, we'll raid the refrigerator and eat some chocolate chip cookie dough, and then we'll sneak into his office and watch *Terminator 2* on his home theater movie screen. It'll be *awesome*."

Everything sounds like fun, I have to admit, except for maybe the cookie dough. That has my stomach feeling a little queasy. Or maybe it's the thought of spending an entire weekend with my should-be-girlfriend's boyfriend.

The whole conversation with JD has me wondering what that niggle wants from me, and if I'm ready to give it.

Jules has her own interpretation, of course, one that she freely gives me every chance she gets. She's especially chatty on the walk home from the bus stop today—this being Friday, the first night of my stay-over at the Tivertons'. She's been rambling on and on about what great friends JD and I could be as I blow some chords on old Gloria. I guess you could say I'm playing a sound track to her thoughts.

I'm not so crazy about those thoughts, incidentally, about me needing more friends and how "JD has more going on than you give him credit for." It's not her words but their rhythm that makes me want to follow along in song.

Jules and I stop to eat a granola bar at Tyler Creek, a tributary of the stream Ma and little Zeb got caught in. Tyler runs clean now that they stopped the mining up on Miller Hill, a testimony to Mother Nature and how she refreshes herself, Papaw once told me. "That doesn't mean that a lot of life didn't die in the process," he was sure to add.

Jules hands me a peanut butter and oats bar her ma made. She knows it's my favorite. We sit on a boulder that's been baking in the sun. As we snack, we listen to the burbling stream and the chip-chip-chipping of chickadees flitting through the branches. Jules crumbles the last of her granola bar and tosses it under a tree, leaving something for the birds like she usually does.

"Curley, what's that?" She sits bolt upright and points several hundred yards up ahead toward a place where the county road peeks through the woods.

I follow her arm up the holler to a line of phosphorescent orange ribbons flashing through the trees. At first, my mind stalls over such an unnatural color in the woods. But then, without a word passing between us, Jules and I jump off our boulder and race toward those ribbons only to confirm what is rising in both of us—our greatest fear.

Tiverton's goons have tramped through the holler, marking all the trees that need to come down to make way for a mining road.

"It's started," I say.

"It's started," she says.

And then we see it. A plastic orange ribbon tied around Ol' Charley. Jules runs and throws her arms around its trunk.

"This can't happen," she sobs.

"I know," I say.

I can feel my heart turning to steel.

Mrs. C says she's going to call up her environmental friends this weekend to see if there's anything they can do about our mountain.

"Curley, I knew Barkley Coal had the lease on Red Hawk, but I never thought they'd do anything with it on account of your family," Mrs. C says before she and Jules leave for the Kmart up in Fraleysburg after dinner. "I was hoping Tiverton might feel the same way." She looks at me with the same sad eyes I've seen on Jules, and I can tell my ma, pa, and little Zeb are all lined up in her mind's eye.

Meanwhile, my duffle bag is packed for JD's, and I don't mind telling you, I'm scared. I've decided my niggle wants me to talk to Mr. Tiverton, to make him see what a bad idea it is to blow up Red Hawk Mountain. I'm afraid I don't have the right words, so I make an emergency call to the only person I know who can get me out of this jam.

"Papaw, I need more words and I need them quick."

Papaw was released from the hospital a few days after my visit and is staying with my Aunt Gertie up in Cincinnati while he recuperates. I talk to him almost every day.

"Hold on there, son. What's all the fuss?"

I tell him about the orange ribbons, spending the week-end at the Tivertons', Jules giving me the word *niggle*, and what I think *my* niggle wants me to do.

"I know it's not Sunday yet, Papaw, but I desperately need my next word to come with me, maybe two."

"Hmmm . . . I see what you mean." He clears his throat. "Curley, you know how I love our system. I love how the alphabet fits so neatly into a year twice over."

"I know, Papaw. But this is an emergency."

"I hear that. I was just going to say that systems, like words, need to remain flexible in order to serve the ones who created them."

"Is that a yes?"

"Yes." And then he gives me *o* and *p*.

I'm good with the *p* word, but what the heck am I supposed to do with *oxymoron*?

"Isn't that a laundry detergent?"

"No." Papaw laughs. "It's a combination of two words or concepts that seem directly opposite each other, like an 'honest lawyer' or a 'loud silence.'"

"How is that going to help?" I practically yell into the phone.

"That's not mine to know," he answers in that obnoxiously mysterious way of his.

I sigh. "Okay, Papaw. Thanks. Gotta go." Sometimes he makes my head hurt.

"Call when you need more, Curley. But make sure you live each word fully. Like gifts and friendship, some words take longer to unwrap."

And some are better left in the box, I want to snap. Thankfully, I catch myself, and we say our good-byes. I hate being short with Papaw, especially now when he's so frail, but the seriousness of what I have to do is squeezing in from all sides. I feel caught in a vise, like the one in Papaw's workshop, and Tiverton Coal is turning the screws.

I hear the kitchen door slam. It's got to be JD. Since he and Jules have been going together, he's like another member of the household. He doesn't even knock. He comes strolling into the living room, where I'm sitting in the dark.

"Hey, Ketchup, what's up?" When I don't answer, he swings my duffle bag over his shoulder and kicks at my feet. "Come on, little brother, let's get going. Looks like you could use some cheering up."

———

I hate to admit it, but Jules is right. There's more to JD than meets the eye.

The first thing he does when we get to his room is show me his Hot Wheels car collection he started as a kid. They're all lined up on a shelf that runs the entire circumference of his room about two feet below the ceiling. There has to be a thousand of them, no kidding. What surprises me most, however, is how uncool it is—I mean, what bad boy admits to having a Hot Wheels car collection?—which, of course, makes him seem that much cooler.

Next, he teaches me the video game *Battle King* like he promised, on his very own gazillion-inch TV. After a few hours, we actually win a battle against some kids from Berlin, which boggles my mind considering our wartime history, not that any of us were alive when it was being made. Now, there's an oxymoron: a friendly battle. Papaw would never believe it.

Around midnight, Mr. Tiverton sticks his head in the room to check on us. He acts all fatherly and concerned about us "staying up too late." JD ignores him and keeps waging war.

"How's your grandpa, Curley?" Mr. Tiverton asks before leaving.

"He's better, sir." *He'd be even better if you weren't about to blow up our mountain.*

"Glad to hear it. We've been thinking about him," he says as he quietly shuts the door.

After that, JD and I watch a really old movie called *Rebel Without a Cause*, starring this bad-boy actor, James Dean, who kind of looks like JD himself. Come to think of it, he even has his initials. According to JD, it's one of the greatest movies ever made, but it seemed kind of hokey to me. The DVD came off a spiral shelf that's floor-to-ceiling movies. There's so many I haven't seen; it would take a year of Sundays to watch them all.

Papaw's always saying how money can't buy happiness, but after my first night at the Tivertons', I'm beginning to think it can.

We stay up until 2:00 a.m. Friday night, which I guess is really Saturday. JD gives me his bed and sleeps on a blow-up mattress by his enormous dresser, a useless piece of furniture since he keeps all his clothes on the floor. Something I hope Jules never finds out about JD and I'm never going to tell her: He snores.

It's noon by the time we wake up. The weekend's half-gone and I'm starting to feel anxious about finding a time for me and Mr. Tiverton to talk. He spends the day either closed up in his office or sitting in front of the TV in the living room watching baseball. "Now that the season's started," JD says, "I'll see even less of him, which is fine by me."

JD wants to play more *Battle King.* The kids from Berlin are online again and calling us to a rematch. Two hours into it, my head starts to ache, what with all the land mines and bombs and hand grenades blowing up in surround sound.

"Can we go outside?" I plead after we lose another battle.

"Outside? What's that?" JD jokes. "Some kind of virtual reality? You hicks are all alike."

We spend the rest of the afternoon playing around with his video camera, filming stuff in the woods near his house from weird angles and making the other one guess what it is. For dinner, we grab a roll of paper towels, a couple of Cokes, and eat pizza up in his room, something that would never happen at my house. Papaw would insist on eating dinner together at the table with our guest. But Mr. Tiverton has to run out to check on one of his mines. He says he'll be back in time for dessert, but JD says, "Don't hold your breath."

"Does it ever feel lonely?" I ask, peeling a piece of pepperoni off the top of the pizza and popping it into my mouth. "I mean, being in this big house all by yourself?"

"Sometimes. But it was worse when Mom and Dad were together." JD tosses me a paper towel and motions for me to dig in. "Up in Indiana, when the 'rents were mad at each other, they'd freeze each other out. You might say I got caught in the cross-freeze. You'd know when things were really bad between them when the house got deadly quiet."

"Like a loud silence?" I ask.

"Yeah, weird, huh?" JD takes a sip of Coke. "You know how I've been saying that Mom's not here because she's waiting for our other house to sell?" I nod. "Well, really, she just can't stand living with the old man. Dad's a workaholic, see. When he was home, he'd shut himself up in his study, even sleep in there. Mom would watch the Shopping Channel and drink." JD shrugs. "Now the only tension in the house is between me and the old man. Mostly, he's so busy, he just lets me be."

It feels like my last bite of pizza's caught halfway down my throat. "So how's your ma doing? How often do you see her?"

"I guess she's doing a lot better now that we're gone. She even got a job doing marketing for a local mall. Ha! I guess you could say all that research on the Shopping Channel paid off."

He stops to roll another piece of pizza up like a burrito, from the point to the crust. I'm marveling at how much food one person can fit in his mouth and still breathe, much less talk, when he adds, "I don't blame her for not coming with us to Hicksville. Living with my old man would drive anyone crazy." He swishes a swig of Coke around in his mouth and swallows hard. "I miss her, though. I only get to see her every few months."

Only twenty-four hours ago, I was envious of JD for his car collection, his big-screen TV, his video camera, his computer, his house, and his games, but now I'm realizing he's as much an orphan as I am. As a matter of fact, the more I'm with JD, the more I see. He's his very own walking oxymoron—an orphan with parents and a good bad boy, if there is such a thing.

I don't know what makes me do it—maybe it's that niggle again, or maybe I feel like it's my turn to share something sad, but I tell JD about the orange ribbons and what his father's planning to do with our mountain.

"I was hoping to talk to him this weekend," I say. "Maybe get him to change his mind." As soon as I say it, I can hear how silly it sounds. How pointless.

But JD isn't laughing. His face is turning red, like he's embarrassed or maybe mad.

"So that's why you came?" He's tearing his paper towel into tiny little wads.

My gut does one of those slow rolls as I realize what I said, or at least how it sounded. I want to blurt out, *I didn't mean it that way!* but something about JD makes me want to tell it straight.

"Yeah, that's why I *thought* I came."

His dark eyebrows knit together in an upside-down V, like I'm one gigantic puzzle.

"I don't get it, either." I think about that dang niggle and silently curse it. "If it's any consolation, Jules thinks I'm here to make friends with you."

His face softens at the mention of her name. "Yeah?"

"Yeah." I chew on a pizza crust, now that I'm pretty sure he's not going to kill me. "She may be right."

———

Oxymoron—*noun*

: a phrase in which the words seem to be in opposition to each other or have contradictory meanings; e. g., *cruel kindness*; *laborious idleness*

My definition: a juxtaposed conundrum that in the right context makes perfect sense

"Are you sure your dad's asleep by now?" I whisper as we creep down the dark hallway.

"Yeah, couldn't you hear him snoring when we went by his bedroom?" JD pauses at a door. "Come on. This is it."

As we pass over the threshold of the door into his father's study, I know I am crossing a line. I am no longer Curley Hines, the quiet and good. I am Curley Hines, the *renegade* (*r* word, last fall), the rebel *with* a cause.

Inside, JD shuts the door and turns on the light. I feel like a mole coming out of its hole in broad daylight. When my eyes finally adjust, I think there must be some mistake. The room looks more like a den than an office. There's a field-stone fireplace in one corner with what appears to be a fully stocked bar beside it. A humongous movie screen takes up most of the wall in an opposite corner facing an over-stuffed couch.

"Over here." JD heads over to his father's desk, which is as long and wide as our kitchen table. On one end, long rolls of paper are stacked in a kind of pyramid. "Surveys of mining sites." JD picks one up. "This could be yours."

The idea that the entire fate of my mountain might be rolled up in that one lousy tube stokes a fire in my gut that may never go out.

"Wait a minute." JD looks at some sketches spread out on the desk, weighed down by books at each corner. "Look here, Curley." *Red Hawk Mountain* is written in blue at the top of the sheet.

"This is it," I whisper. My voice comes out all raspy. Fear grips me from the inside out.

Parallel lines reveal the mining road that runs through the holler and up the mountain, beginning at the county road, just like Jules and I saw yesterday. More lines cut through the center figure that represents Red Hawk Mountain, with numbers off to the side indicating elevation.

"That's where the coal is." JD points. "Each line shows how much of the mountain will be taken down to get to the coal deposit, one slice at a time." The engineer's drawing looks so delicate and precise, it's eerie, considering what our mountain will look like a year from now if all goes according to Tiverton's plan.

JD grabs a black datebook from the center drawer and holds it up.

"Hey, Ketchup. This should tell us something."

He opens it to today's date and starts thumbing through the rest of April as I look over his shoulder. On April 21, which is a little over a week away, it reads: *R.H. access road*. I'm guessing the *R.H.* stands for Red Hawk.

"That's when Ol' Charley's coming down, I bet," I say, pointing at the date. We start flipping through more days, when we hear the sound of a toilet flushing on the other side of the wall.

"Shhhh! The old man!"

JD scrambles from behind the desk and pulls me toward the couch. Grabbing a remote from the entertainment cabinet, he points it at the screen. We're after the lesser of two evils here, as Papaw would say, but my heart's still thumping like a rabbit against the walls of a cage.

"Boys?" Mr. Tiverton leans against the doorframe, dressed in gray flannel pajamas, his short-cropped hair standing up helter-skelter in all directions. "What's the meaning of this?"

JD casually turns toward his father as if he just noticed him. "Oh, hi, Dad. Sorry if we woke you up. We were just about to watch a movie."

His father glances around the room. "Isn't it a little late for that?" He walks over to his desk and shuffles through some papers.

I try not to watch his every move. I try to relax.

"What's wrong with *your* TV?"

"Your screen has higher def, and, well . . . it's bigger," JD quips.

I'm beginning to think we're in the clear, when out of the corner of my eye, I notice Mr. Tiverton pick up his date-book and study it. JD didn't have time to put it back in the drawer.

"Boys?" Mr. Tiverton's voice is deadly calm. "Can you explain what my calendar is doing on my desk and not in the drawer where I always keep it?"

You know how they say that before an accident, everything seems to go in slow motion? Well, that's how it is for me in this moment, when I know I'm about to come clean. My *p* word comes to me in Papaw's voice, sending me strength. It's like having a superpower. I feel electrified when I think it.

Persist.

JD starts to make something up, but I wave him off. "That's okay, JD, I've got this."

I stand in front of Mr. Tiverton and his enormous desk. "I looked at it, sir. I wanted to know what your plan was for Red Hawk Mountain."

He sets the book down. "I see."

"I apologize for sneaking in here like this. It's not how my papaw raised me. But when I saw those orange ribbons the other day on all those trees, well, I felt desperate about saving them. And my mountain, too, of course."

Mr. Tiverton sits down in his office chair and leans over the blueprints like he might just lay his head down and go to sleep. "Curley . . . your grandfather and I have already talked about this."

"Yes, sir, I know. But you haven't talked with me. I'm pretty sure my words aren't going to make a lick of difference, but Papaw says it's the trying that counts."

Mr. Tiverton leans back in his chair with his arms crossed tightly over his chest. I look over at JD, who is now lounging on the couch, his legs dangling over one arm. I can't see his face, but I can see his bare feet swinging freely, and for some reason, that steadies me.

Persist.

"Red Hawk Mountain means the world to me. It *is* my world. It's all I've ever known from the time I was knee-high to a rooster. I'm sure I've walked every inch of it. I know it like the back of my hand. All my memories of my daddy and Ma and little Zeb are rooted there with the trees. I wake up to that mountain. I go to sleep to that mountain. Some days I might not think about it or even appreciate it, but it's always there, kind of like God. You take that mountain away from me and Papaw, and you might as well take our house, too. The mountain is our home."

JD's feet have stopped swinging, which pretty much tells me he's heard every word. Mr. Tiverton just sits there and stares. Finally, he says, "Are you finished?"

"Yes, sir. I am." I thought for sure I was going to need some of the words Papaw gave me, but I guess I had enough of my own.

"Curley, you probably think I'm a man without a heart." He throws a quick glance toward the couch. "That's what some people in this house think, anyway. But I know your story and your papaw's, too, and they move me. I didn't need to continue that deal you had with Barkley Coal, but I did, didn't I?"

I nod. "Yes, sir. And we're thankful for it."

"I kept that deal, because I care about what happens to you, Curley." He's speaking so softly I have to step closer to hear him. "Coal takes care of its own. *That's* why I need to mine this mountain. I have employees and their families to consider. If I didn't move forward with this lease, I'd have to start laying people off. I also wouldn't have the money to keep up with the causes I care about most, if you catch my drift."

He rubs his face with his hands, as if he might wipe away all that responsibility, which, I've got to admit, sounds like a lot. Still, it feels funny to be called a "cause," although Carl Jenkins once called me a lost one.

"In case you're listening, JD"—Mr. Tiverton's tone takes on an edge—"it's my job that's on the line, too. Tiverton Coal pays for *this* house and *your* video games and *your* college education, if you should be so lucky to have one."

JD flips his legs off the couch and springs toward the door. "Yeah, well, maybe I don't need you or your money." Turning toward me, he says, "I told you this would be absolutely futile." It's the same word I used at Ma and Zeb's funeral, when I threw that shovel down.

"Come on, Curley," JD says. "Let's get out of here."

"Not so fast, you two." The edge to Mr. Tiverton's voice grows sharper with every word. "We're not quite done here."

His piercing look shoots right through me, and I realize I need to pee. The urge is so bad, I squeeze my legs together like a little kid.

"First of all, there's no excuse for you boys breaking into my office and going through my desk. That was a terrible violation," he says.

"You mean, like blowing the top off a mountain?" I can't believe I say that *out loud*. Judging from the look on JD's face, he can't believe it, either.

If words carry weight like Papaw says they do, then silence must weigh more than a dictionary, or at least that's how heavy it feels standing in front of Mr. Tiverton like this, with him just staring. I fully expect him to unleash his wrath and, while he's at it, send me out into the pitch-black night, but he drops his head into his hands and sighs. When he finally looks up, I'd swear he looks more raggedy than Papaw did after his bypass surgery.

"Curley, I know you came here hoping to change my mind, and I guess I don't blame you. But there are things you kids simply don't understand. Things that come first in this life—

yes, even before mountains. And that's jobs and putting food on the table and making sure folks have enough energy to heat their houses on cold winter nights. Maybe you think I'm in some kind of dirty business, but I'm working my tail off here to help keep this country running. Almost forty percent of this country's electricity—and more than eighty percent of the electricity in the Commonwealth of Kentucky alone—runs on coal. If it doesn't come from your mountain, where's it going to come from?"

I want to say, *Somebody else's mountain*, but I can't seem to work out the justice of that. Besides, my brain is having a hard time concentrating, what with having to pee and all. I mean, I'm seeing yellow.

"Look here, Curley, I'm a businessman . . ."

JD groans. His dad shoots him a poison-dart glare before turning back to me.

". . . and as such, my first duty is to protect my business at all costs. Tiverton Coal will be mining Red Hawk Mountain; it's as simple as that. Do you understand?"

Mr. Tiverton peers into my eyes, as if willing me to come to my senses. Maybe he thinks he's made a case for Big Coal. But where I come from? All the good sense in the world will never add up to a mountain.

"Honestly, sir?" I say. "I *don't.*" And then I turn and run.

"Man, Ketchup, that took some *swag*," JD whisper-shouts as we scramble down the hall.

I turn into the bathroom closest to his room, one of five in the house I've counted so far. As I pee, I think of my *p* word. Who would have ever guessed that such a simple word could be so risky? And what will it *mean*?

The loss of everything?

———————

Persist—*verb*

: to stand firm; to be fixed and unmoved; to stay; to continue steadfastly; especially, to continue fixed in a course of conduct against opposing motives; to persevere

Q and R

*Gurrrrrruuup! Rrrrrrrrrrr . . . zing! Rrrrrrrrr . . . up, up, up . . .
zzzziiiing! Zzzzzzzzzziiiiiiing!*

The holler rings with high-powered chain saws ripping a
path through the woods. A bulldozer follows closely behind,
banging against uprooted trunks like a bull butting its head
against a fence post, only this bull never yields. Everything
gives way in the end.

"Curley!" Jules screams as she tears through the woods,
outpacing both me and JD. "They're almost there!"

A tree moans mere yards from where we're running,
then . . . CRACK! It crashes to the ground. There's a gentle
whooooooosh of green-leafed branches coming to rest and
then . . . nothing. No birds. No rustling of leaves in the wind.
Just the smell of fresh wood, a fatal wound.

*Gurrrrrruuup! Rrrrrrrrrrr . . . zing! Rrrrrrrrr . . . up, up,
up . . . zzzziiiing!*

164

"Come on, you two," JD yells as Jules and I throw our backpacks against the trunk of our favorite tree. "I'll give you a hand up."

Jules and I settle onto our favorite branch of Ol' Charley, straddling him like the horse we've imagined him to be. I'd say it was like old times, but old times were never like this. In the olden days, we never had a bulldozer or an army of chain saws breathing down our necks, much less a third party watching our every move. This last part was planned, mind you. Still, I'd rather be alone with Jules any day.

JD pulls a stack of signs made out of poster board from Jules's backpack and hands them up to her. Then he starts fiddling with his video camera.

"Give me a sec," he says, "and we'll be ready to roll."

I turn to give Jules a thumbs-up, and see that she's crying.

"What's wrong?" I immediately feel stupid for asking.

Thankfully, she ignores me and wipes her face with her jacket sleeve. "Curley?"

I nod, daring to look into her eyes.

"I'll be strong for you if you'll be strong for me," she says, holding her little finger in the air between us. "Deal?"

I hook my pinkie around hers and shake.

"Deal."

Not only can I feel the strength of our friendship in that silly kid's pledge, but also the strength of my new resolve. I will do anything to save our mountain. And the fight starts here.

"Hey, you kids! We need you out of that tree. Now!" A man who appears to be the crew boss yells at us, cradling a massive chain saw across his chest. The rest of his cronies gather around him. They're all wearing bright orange jackets with TIVERTON COAL emblazoned in black across their backs.

"Sorry, sir, we're doing homework here!" I yell in reply. It's a stall tactic, but, hopefully, it will buy us some time.

"Homework? In a tree?" The guy chortles at his buddies. "Kids these days, eh?" They all laugh. "Reminds me of that song we used to sing in school. 'Susie and Johnny sitting in a tree, K-I-S-S-I-N-G!'" He sings off-key. "Sure it's homework you're doing?"

Jules flashes him a big smile. "Yeah, we're making a little movie here for a class project. We need about half an hour. Can you give us that?"

He looks up at us and shrugs. "Aw, I guess there's no harm

in taking a break." He looks over at JD. "Hey! Aren't you Tiverton's kid?"

"Yes, sir. At least on the days he claims me." The men laugh. JD's got that good-old-boy thing down pat. "We're on the same science team," he adds, motioning to Jules and me up in the tree.

"I see." The boss studies JD for a minute, then waves at the bulldozer guy to shut off his engine. "Hey, Gordy. Stay here and keep an eye on things, would you? When we get back in half an hour, kids, you'd better be gone. This is no place for playing around." Then he signals the rest of his crew to follow him back to the county road, where a line of trucks is parked.

Gordy is a big man with a head as bald as a buzzard's and biceps the size of cows. He might be as nice as your Aunt Sally, but he looks like he'd just as soon grind you up as say "Excuse me" if you got in his way. Papaw's wood chipper comes to mind.

"Don't worry about me," he shouts over at us. "I'll just be hanging out here admiring the view." He stretches his arms up and folds them under his head, leaning back in his seat. He's wearing one of those jean shirts with the sleeves ripped out. The dragon tattoos on his arms look like they're breathing, ready to torch anything in their path.

"Ignore him, you guys," JD says. "As long as you talk in a normal voice, Curley, he won't be able to hear what you're saying. This camera has a super sensitive mike that will pick you up just fine." JD looks through the viewfinder and says, "Ready?"

"Hold on, JD." I'm breaking out in a cold sweat. "Give me a minute to check my notes." As I shuffle through my cards, Jules arranges the stack of signs on her lap.

This video we're about to make? We're going to post it on the Internet to tell the world what's happening to our mountain. Mr. A says we're tilting at windmills, an expression that comes from a novel about this crazy guy, Don Quixote, who wages battles against imaginary foes. Quixote is just a character in a book, but he became so famous they named a word after him—my q word for the week, *quixotic*. I figure Papaw was inspired by Mr. A himself, now that the two friends are talking again.

Mr. A says he'll do anything he can to support our project, regardless of how idealistic it sounds. "I'll even commit a subversive act or two, if it'll help the cause," he said. We considered asking him to cut the ribbons off the trees, but we knew he'd do it, and we're trying to keep everyone out of jail.

As the self-proclaimed director, JD has the whole project mapped out in his head. The only change he made to my script was to replace *my* with *our* when I'm talking about Red Hawk Mountain. "It's Jules's mountain, too," he said, "and people will want to know you're in this fight together. They'll look at the two of you up in that old tree and think, 'How cute,' 'How sweet,' 'I wonder if they're in love.' And we want them thinking that, see? Love sells." Jules and I both blushed when he said that.

I'm blushing now just thinking about it, when I notice her smiling at me.

"You're going to do great," she says, and there's that dimple again. I tuck my notes out of sight. She's right. I have everything I need.

"Okay, JD. We're ready up here."

"Okay, then . . . *Action!*" JD slices his arm through the air and I begin.

"Curley Hines here. This is my best friend, Jules. And this is our tree." I hear the camera zoom out, probably from a close-up of me and Jules to a wide shot of the tree. "We call our tree Ol' Charley, after a horse. And that up there is Red

Hawk Mountain." I point behind me. "We've lived here all our lives.

"We're coming to you from Wonder Gap, Kentucky, and as you can see, we're in a bit of a pickle." JD pans from us to the bulldozer. Good old Gordy is glaring in our direction. Maybe it's just the sun, but fortunately for our purposes, he looks as mean as a junkyard dog.

"That bulldozer wants to run right over Ol' Charley here—a tree that is important to the Cherokee and over three hundred years old. For once in my life, I refuse to *acquiesce*."

Jules holds up her first sign: ACQUIESCE: GIVE IN. She cocks her head, and her dark, curly hair loops over one corner of the poster board like a parenthesis, and I almost forget everything I'm about to say. I clear my throat.

"My papaw's been giving me a word a week for as long as I can remember, and he's taught me to use my words for good. So if you think I'm being *belligerent*, well, then . . . I've got a reason to be."

Jules holds up: BELLIGERENT: AT WAR, READY TO FIGHT.

"You see, I've been working on a *conundrum* that I need your help to solve. This is no time to *dillydally*, so I'll come right to the point."

Jules looks over her DILLYDALLY sign and winks at me, like she's shooting me the memory of that time with the elk. I grin at that wink—I can't help myself, even though I'm supposed to be all serious about what comes next in my speech. I hope like heck JD can cut out these pauses and tighten up the speech like he says he can. I take one look at Gordy the dozer guy and drop my smile.

"That bulldozer there belongs to Tiverton Coal. Not only does Tiverton Coal want to run over Ol' Charley, but they want to *eradicate* every living thing on Red Hawk Mountain. That's right. After they put in this mining road, they're going to burn down all the trees, which will kill or scatter all the critters, of course. And then they're going to blow up our mountain. That's right, blow up our mountain. I'm not kidding. Right here in our backyard. This is what it would look like." Jules holds up a picture of the mountaintop removal site JD clipped from the video I shot on the elk tour.

"They used to call this kind of mining *mountaintop removal*. Now the industry calls it *Appalachian surface coal mining*."

Jules's next sign says: HUH?

"Now, I'm as *fallible* as the next guy, but I'm not *gullible*. Surface is one thing. This mountaintop is GONE."

"Can you imagine Mount Everest without its top?"

Jules holds up a picture of a topless Mount Everest, photoshopped by JD.

"I'll say this: It takes a lot of *hutzpah* to blow the top off a mountain, but mountaintop removal is *irrevocable*. When a mountaintop is gone, it's gone for good." Jules rests her chin on the edge of the IRREVOCABLE sign. There's no denying the sadness in her eyes.

"Papaw says that sometimes, when you *juxtapose* two things, you can see something you didn't see before. So just in case I haven't been clear: Here's our mountain as it is today." Jules holds up a photo of Red Hawk. "And here's what used to be a mountain." Jules puts the mining site picture and our mountain side by side.

"Can you imagine waking up one morning and seeing this?" I point to the mining photo. "Who was the *kleptomaniac* who stole my mountain?" Jules shrugs and flips the poster board, revealing: KLEPTOMANIAC: THIEF.

"Our mountain is the *linchpin* that holds our lives together. That's a powerful *metaphor*, and it points to the truth. Blow the top off Red Hawk Mountain and life as we know it falls apart."

The seriousness of the situation hits me real sudden like, and I freeze. Jules grabs my hand, and I can feel this bolt of energy zing right through me, like a car battery getting a jump. I stare into the camera and try to concentrate on talking to that one person who will care enough to act. Papaw says that's all it takes.

"So what can *you* do? Well, while Jules and I are sitting up here on Ol' Charley, you could be using *your* words for good. You could write a letter to your newspaper or representative. You could send a link to this video to your friends or your local TV station. Or you could come on down to Wonder Gap, Kentucky, and sit with us on our mountain. There's nowhere in the world more beautiful to be.

"Can you feel it? You know, that finger in your gut that's poking you to do something? Jules calls that a *niggle*." Jules grins as she pulls up her next sign: NIGGLE: A THOUGHT THAT BUGS YOU. "If you're feeling a niggle, then don't just sit there, do something. Say something. Let us know you're listening. We need to know you care.

"Tiverton Coal is not all-powerful. Only God is. That's what Papaw says. But Papaw also says that when we come together for good, we can be powerful beyond measure. We're

173

not asking you to save the world, or Appalachia, for that matter. We're asking you to help us save our mountain." Jules nods, and I realize I have never felt closer to her in my life.

"A topless mountain is an *oxymoron*. But with your support, we will *persist*."

After holding up OXYMORON and PERSIST, Jules lets the cards fall from the tree, leaving her empty-handed and looking a bit lost. This time I'm the one offering *her* a hand, and she takes it. I guess we're selling that love thing. I look at JD and wonder what he sees.

"With your support," I say to the camera, "we can save our mountain."

A distant slamming of doors punctuates my final words. Jules and I look out from our vantage point on Ol' Charley. We can hear voices shouting at us from the woods near the road, one rising above the others.

"JD! What do you think you're doing!"

Mr. Tiverton.

He's practically flying through the trees. JD calmly moves the camera from its focus on Jules and me to his father and the angry men in orange crashing through the underbrush, heading our way.

"Looks like we've got company," he says.

Whirrrr. The lens retracts as he fiddles with the camera then roots around his pockets like he's looking for a place to hide it. Jules is holding my hand so tightly, her fingernails bite into my palm.

"Gimme that thing." Mr. Tiverton yanks the video camera from JD's grasp.

"Chill out, man. I'm not *armed*."

"The heck you're not. What do you call this?" His father shoves the camera an inch from JD's face, then pulls it back, replaying our recent footage on the camcorder's screen. "I'd say you're armed and loaded." Mr. Tiverton drops his arm to his side like the camera all of a sudden gets too heavy to hold. "For crying out loud, JD, you're my *son*!"

Papaw says there's nothing worse than watching a grown man cry, which is what I'm afraid we're about to see when JD says the unthinkable.

"Not like I chose to be."

Jules lets go of my hand and leans forward, as if she might jump. She could, too. I've seen her do it.

"Oh, that's fine. That's just fine." Mr. Tiverton shakes his head and stares at the ground, like JD didn't say what we thought he said, like he told his father to "have a nice day." But then, with absolutely no warning, Mr. Tiverton cocks his arm like he's going to land a punch and slams the camera against our tree.

Jules and I cringe. I expect to see the camera break into a million pieces, but only a few go flying. The bulk of it ricochets off Ol' Charley like he's some kind of rubber tree and lands at the crew boss's feet.

JD snickers, his father lunges, and I'm afraid we're about to witness a murder.

Mr. Tiverton pulls JD forward by his jacket collar to within an inch of his face. Their noses are so much alike— long and straight to the tip—they look like mirror images of each other, except for JD's nose ring, of course.

"You, you . . ." Mr. Tiverton's mouth is all scrunched up, like he's trying to find just the right word to call his son.

Gordy the dozer guy coughs. Still holding JD in his grip, Mr. Tiverton looks around at his men. "Get out of here, all of you," he yells over his shoulder. "You can take this tree down first thing Monday when these kids are in school."

Mr. Tiverton gives JD one more look of disbelief before he opens his hand and lets him drop. His fingers remain curved and stiff like claws until the foreman hands him the dinged-up camera.

"And *you*, Mr. Hines." Mr. Tiverton shakes the camera at me like a fist. "You're making it awfully hard for me to think kindly toward you. I think you know what I mean."

"I do." My voice is trembling so bad, I'm not even sure he hears it.

Mr. Tiverton turns to follow his men out of the woods, but then stops as if he's forgotten something. "JD? You coming?" he snaps.

"Naw," JD says, waving him off like he's some kind of afterthought. "I'll get a ride from Mrs. C." His voice sounds casual, even cheery—as if his dad didn't almost kill him, as if our only chance to tell the world about our plight hadn't just been smashed to smithereens.

"Suit yourself." Mr. Tiverton trudges off, leaving emptiness in his wake.

"Good thing Papaw also gave me *resilience* this week," I grumble to Jules as we climb down from Ol' Charley. "I think we're going to need it."

———————

"So . . . what's plan B?" Jules breaks the silence as we arrive back at her trailer.

JD's grinning like a sack full of possum heads, as Papaw would say, and for the life of me, I can't figure out why. He reaches into his pocket.

"Plan B!" he announces, whipping out this itty-bitty square thing about the size of a postage stamp and waving it over his head.

"My hero!" Jules shouts, yanking on his arm.

"Would someone please fill me in on what just happened?" My brain still feels a bit *addled* (*a* word, fifth grade), what with losing the video and all.

"It's called a memory card, Curley, my boy." JD holds it in front of my face between his thumb and index finger. "Before the old man got to the camera, I saved our movie on it. It's a backup to the one that's still in the camera. My old man has no clue there were two."

When it finally dawns on me that all is not lost, we high-five each other until our palms are sore, and then we start chanting, "Plan B! Plan B! Plan B!" while jumping up and down all in a bunch like we're basketball stars who just won the national championship. I'm thinking about my word for the week—how *resilience* is a memory card—when JD sinks that little puppy into the palm of my hand.

"Now all we need is a subversive act," he says. "Know where we can get one?"

————

Quixotic—*adjective*

: like Don Quixote; romantic to extravagance; absurdly chivalric; apt to be deluded

Resilience—*noun*

: an ability to be flexible, to recover or adapt after a difficult change or experience

You might think *subversive* is my word for the week, but it isn't even close. I seriously doubt if Papaw would consider it a helpful word, much less approve of the activity, which is why Mr. Amons says it would be best not to tell him.

As I've mentioned before, I've pretty much been a good kid all my life. I get good grades, I do my chores, and I address my elders with respect. Yet here I am—prowling through the halls of Blue Ridge Middle School on a Saturday night, my heart pounding, my armpits sticky, taking part in a covert operation with a subversive science teacher and my two best friends.

As JD would say, what's not to like about that?

Never mind that Mr. A has keys.

"Okay, you guys. You're here for extra credit, right?" Mr. A unlocks the door to the computer lab and switches on the lights. "If anyone finds out what we're really doing, I could lose my job."

"Don't worry, Mr. A. We've got you covered." Jules gives him a thumbs-up as JD and I rush to the closest computer and turn it on.

I'm flabbergasted at how simple it is. We've already decided not to make any changes to the footage. "Leaving it raw keeps it real," JD says. So we click on the website You2CanChangetheWorld.com, enter some basic information about the video, insert the memory card, and we're ready to post.

My words.

Into the universe.

Like scattered stars.

"W-w-w-wait," I stammer.

"Wait for what?" Jules whispers, so close her breath tickles my ear.

"What if no one sees it?" I say. "Oh my gosh, what if they do?"

"That's what we want." JD puts a hand on my shoulder. "Go ahead, Ketchup, hit POST."

The resulting click barely makes a sound at all.

"Congratulations!" the screen announces. "You, too, can change the world!"

"Move over, Curley." Jules skootches me over and grabs the mouse. I can feel the warmth of her hip against mine. She closes out of the site, only to click back in. She says she wants to get a feel for what it will be like for "our people," as she calls them, to view our video for the first time. She searches for our title.

"There it is!" She clicks on it. *Topless in Wonder Gap.*

Okay, so that was JD's idea. He'd come up with it right after we celebrated plan B.

"A title is everything," he said. "It's the hook. Trust me, it'll grab people's attention."

Trust him?

"Okay," I said, "with one condition. We add a subtitle: *Help Us Save Our Mountain.*"

We all watch our video together, huddled around the computer screen. "Oh my gosh, Curley, you're brilliant," Jules gushes. It's like the fifth time she's said that.

"Watch this, Mr. A." I can feel JD nudge our teacher behind my back. It's the part near the end where I offer Jules my hand. "Curley really drives it home here."

"Aha . . ." Mr. A says.

I glance over at Jules, who has become perfectly still. The computer screen casts a bluish light on her face, and I wonder what she's thinking. I desperately want to take her hand. I mean, it's right there under the desk, but JD's standing behind us and, well, he's my friend.

You would think that would make things easier.

After we watch JD's father come raging through the woods and close out the video, we check the number of views it has so far.

The counter says: 2.

"Two?!" The three of us kids scream.

"That means . . ." Jules pauses.

"Somebody else has watched it besides us." Mr. A finishes her sentence.

But . . . who?

———————————

The next day, I call Papaw up in Cincinnati and tell him that JD, Jules, and I are going to need a big dose of luck getting anybody to watch our video, much less help us save our mountain. "You don't need luck," he says. "You need *serendipity*." When I look up its definition, however, I honestly don't see the difference, so I call him back.

"Luck is luck," I tell him, twirling the springy cord on the Cavanaughs' kitchen phone. Mrs. C is out visiting a friend, Jules is locked away in her room studying for a history exam, and I'm feeling as lonely for Papaw as a hound left home from the hunt.

"Curley, you should know better than that by now," he answers in a husky voice. His voice is so much stronger now. "A word is never 'just' one thing or another."

"Right, Papaw. How could I forget?" I wonder if he can hear me smiling.

"For one thing, *serendipity* suggests something *pleasant* happening unexpectedly. *Luck*, on the other hand, can be either good or bad."

"And for another?" I egg him on.

"When you look at its origin, *serendipity* also suggests that this 'happy accident' happens as a result of a search—when one is looking for one thing but is surprised to discover something else."

"Kind of like how I was looking for Jules to be my girlfriend, but instead I discovered a friend in the person I thought I hated?" Judging from the long pause, I'm pretty sure Papaw never expected to hear this.

"So . . . did that surprise you?" he finally asks.

"As JD would say . . . Heck, *yeah!*"

Papaw laughs. "Well, that's *serendipity*."

———————

Our next subversive act happens on Monday, two days after we post our video. This time it will be just me and Jules up in Ol' Charley staging a "sit-in," as Mrs. C likes to call it. JD will be in school on account of his father making sure he gets there.

"That's all right," he tells us over the phone at seven in the morning. "This way I can check to see how many views we're getting. Man, I hope I'm watching when it goes viral. Dudes! That would be *awesome*." JD thinks that all of his cyber networking is going to make a difference, but Jules and I have our doubts. Still, his enthusiasm is contagious. When we hang up, Jules and I look at each other and laugh.

"That boy," Jules says, and I know exactly what she means.

We have Mrs. C's permission to miss school, and Papaw's, too. "Our country was founded by renegades," Papaw told me over the phone last night. "What you're doing will be far more educational than anything they can teach you in civics class."

Jules and I climbed up into Ol' Charley at 7:30 this

morning, making sure we'd be here before the "chain saw massacre," or so Jules calls Tiverton's road crew. Mrs. C has given us a day's supply of food and drink and an old horse blanket for a cushion. Nevertheless, after an hour of straddling our branch, my butt feels like it's been sitting on a nest of porcupines. Subversion can be *hard*.

The road crew guys trudge right past us when they arrive, giving us dirty looks. I guess they've been told to skip over Ol' Charley for now and head on up the mountain. Mr. Tiverton probably figures we'll give up eventually, which, in case you're wondering, isn't going to happen. Besides, it's a beautiful day in Wonder Gap. Jules and I watch as the morning mist slips through the holler like somebody's tugging on the bedsheets farther down. Redbuds and dogwoods speckle the new-green woods around us with dashes of purple and white. Even though my bottom hurts, there's no place else I'd rather be— and no one else I'd rather be with.

And then the whine of chain saws fills the air. The sound reminds me of the screaming banshees Mama used to warn me about when I was a little boy. She'd demonstrate by making this high-pitched screeching sound, chasing me around the house to my own high-pitched squeals of laughter. She said the banshees haunted the woods at night, just waiting to gobble somebody up. I'm pretty sure all of that was to keep me from wandering off, and it worked.

Jules winces at every crashing tree.

We are greeted by a number of visitors throughout the day, some expected, some not. Gordy the dozer guy is our first. His dragons seem even more ferocious in the morning light.

"Hey, you kids!" he yells, chomping into an apple and making half of it disappear.

Jules pulls out the pepper spray her ma gave us just in case.

"What you guys are doing up there?" He takes one more bite and tosses the core into the woods. "It takes a lot of guts." I let out a breath I didn't know I was holding.

"My daddy was one of those hippy protestors back in the seventies. He marched on Washington during the Vietnam War." His barrel chest seems to expand with pride as he tells us about his pa and how he became a conscientious objector and all. When we offer him a turn in our tree, he laughs and spits out a few apple seeds.

"Well, that would be job suicide, now, wouldn't it? I've got kids to feed." He tosses us a couple of apples out of his lunch pail before he goes back to work. "Those are from our orchard, incidentally. Might be a few worms. They won't hurt you none."

Sometime around noon, Clay Whitaker, the local sheriff, ambles through the woods and sidles up to the tree like he's on some kind of social call, although I'm pretty sure he's come to take us to jail. We've been expecting him all morning. His mother is Cherokee, though. So I'm hoping he feels some kinship with Ol' Charley and will show us some mercy.

"Well, looky here, you two. You've got yourselves into quite a fix, I see."

"With all due respect, Sheriff, I'd say it's Red Hawk Mountain that's in a fix, wouldn't you?" Jules tosses her apple core into the woods behind her. "Not to mention this tree."

The sheriff hooks his thumbs into his gun belt and rocks on his feet. "Yup, I guess you could say that. Yup, I guess you could." I'm wondering if he's trying to catch us off guard by lulling us to sleep with all that rocking, when he finally gets to his point.

"Kids, here's the thing. The law's the law. Tiverton Coal has a permit that gives them the right to take down this tree, and you're obstructing that right. Not to mention, you belong in school."

Jules and I look at each other and shrug.

He picks up a long stick and starts poking at some leaves. "I'll never forget the day I pulled your ma and little Zeb out of that riverbank, Curley. I still have nightmares about it."

"Yes, sir. So do I." Jules looks at me in surprise. I've never told her about the nightmares, and I tell her almost everything.

"You and Jules aren't coming out of that tree, are you?" Sheriff Whitaker asks.

"No, sir." Jules answers for both of us. My head's still stuck in those bad dreams.

"Well, I figure you've had your share of suffering on account of coal, Curley Hines. I just don't have it in me to pull you down." He taps the trunk of Ol' Charley twice with the stick and starts to walk away. "You kids be careful up there."

He stops and turns around about midway to the county road. "I'll be sure to tell my ma what you're doing here," he shouts. "She'll be sending you a blessing for sure."

Our next visitor comes walking up the path with Mrs. C. It's about three in the afternoon, as close as I can tell by the sun's slant on the mountain. Jules and I have spelled each other with pee breaks recently, but the excitement of hanging out in a tree all day—even with Jules—is wearing thin.

"Hey, guys, how's it going?" a young woman with spiky blond hair calls up to us. "I'm Regina Hopkins, a photographer from the *Lexington Record*. Someone sent us an anonymous tip this morning about what you kids are doing down here in Wonder Gap, and my editor wanted me to check it out. Mind if I take some pictures?"

"Gosh, no," is all I can manage.

"I wonder who gave them the tip," Jules says, and then looks down at her mother. Standing a few feet behind the reporter, Mrs. C sneaks a wave over her shoulder.

"Never mind," Jules says, scrunching her hair with both hands. For the life of me, I'll never understand why she does that. "How do I look?"

"Fine, I guess?" She scowls at me, and we hear *kishh kishh kishh*.

"Thanks, you two." Regina Hopkins is already putting her camera back in its case. "I think I got the shot." Wait. What? Jules was frowning at me. "It was perfect. You both looked kind of mad."

"I gave her the link to your video," Mrs. C calls over her shoulder as the photographer follows her out of the woods.

"Okay, cool, thanks for coming!" Jules waves after them and then turns around and hits me on the arm.

"Ow! What's that for?"

"For ruining my one chance at fame!"

That's when I pull out my harmonica to ease my nerves, like I've done throughout the day. I'm wailing on my own soulful version of "Stairway to Heaven" by Led Zeppelin from one of Papaw's old rock albums, when Jules reaches over and grabs old Gloria right out of my hands.

"Honestly, Curley. I don't know which is worse," she says, "that song or the sound of all those saws." I'm guessing she thinks it's me.

Now I know what Papaw means when he says he's "reached his boiling point." I'm so mad at Jules for knocking the only thing that's bringing me peace, I could spit hot lava. I never thought I'd say this, but after eight hours with Jules in this God-forsaken tree? I'm ready to be anywhere else.

We spend the next hour not saying another word to each other, a much different kind of silence than what we used to share up here in Ol' Charley before the chain saws came.

By the time Gordy and the rest of the crew pack up their gear for the day, my anger has long since cooled, but every muscle in my body is now as stiff as a poker. Jules and I climb down from Ol' Charley and hobble like eighty-year-olds back to her place.

What we find there boggles the mind.

Her living room, with seating for about three, is packed as tight as a can of sardines with people I don't recognize. Mrs. C is passing around peanut butter cookies and steaming hot cups of sassafras tea.

"Our heroes!" someone shouts as Jules and I walk in to applause.

"Here, guys, take my seat." A tall man with a gray mustache and beard jumps out of a chair brought in from the kitchen.

"No, thank you, sir," I say as Jules and I wave him off. "We've been sitting all day."

Everyone laughs.

"What's going on, Mom?" Jules asks, a bit sharply. I can't blame her. All she's been talking about for the last few hours is taking a hot shower.

"Well, darling . . . for starters, I invited a few of my environmental friends." Several folks smile and wave. "I thought it was time we got organized."

The man with the gray beard speaks up again. "Some of us here have watched your video. We had no idea this was going on in Wonder Gap. We've felt so helpless against the mining industry for so long; some of us are weary from a fight we never seem to win. But your youth and enthusiasm have inspired us. We want to help you save your mountain."

The others in the room clap and nod.

"Some of these folks and others who couldn't be here tonight have offered to take turns sitting in your tree for you," Mrs. C says, "when you want to take a break or . . . heaven forbid . . . go to school." Folks laugh.

"Actually, after an entire day of tree sitting," I say, "school sounds pretty good to me."

Jules raises her hand to give me a high five, something we practiced early on in our tree today. Jules says the key is to focus on the other person's elbow. It sounds like that would throw you off, but no kidding, it works every time.

"We also have a very special guest this evening, and we are honored to have her with us." Mrs. C nods to an older, thin-faced woman sitting across the room in front of us. Long, silver hair streams down her back, a back as straight as an oak plank Papaw might use for a table. There's something familiar about her dark eyes. They look like Sheriff Whitaker's. Could this be . . . ?

"Thank you, Irene." The woman bows. She grips her walking cane and pulls herself up. All eyes in the room watch, and no one makes a sound. It's a moment full of waiting.

"My name is Helen Whitaker. I am Cherokee and a member of the Bird Clan. My ancestors named this sacred mountain you are trying to save Tsiwodi, which means 'hawk.' When my son, Clay, came to see me today, he was quite troubled. He had just talked with these two young people and heard the fire in their plea. 'Ma,' he begged me, 'there must be something the tribe can do to help save Red Hawk Mountain and our Cherokee tree.' That's when I knew my ancestors were calling me: Helen, it's time."

She motions for Jules and me to walk toward her. People sitting on the floor scoot back, clearing the way. I know this sounds weird, but it feels like we're walking down an aisle, you know, to get married. She reaches out and we take her hands. They are long-fingered and wrinkled, but her grip is strong. A large silver-and-turquoise ring in the shape of a turtle twists around her index finger and rests on top of my hand. She waits until she has drawn my gaze into hers. I want to look over at Jules to see what she's doing or what she thinks, but the old woman makes that impossible.

"That tree, my young friends—the one I hear you call Ol' Charley—has witnessed the plight of my people for over three hundred years. My ancestors hid in that tree to escape removal, when so many of us were forced to walk the Trail of Tears, or as the Cherokee call it, the Trail Where They Cried. The tree is part of our legacy, and it stands as a sentinel to a sacred site." Her words create a stir in the room. Does she mean the mountain? I never thought of it as sacred, but I guess it could be. And then she adds, "An ancient burial site." Whispers float around us as Jules and I stand calm in Mrs. Whitaker's dark-eyed gaze. She waits. When the room grows quiet again, she continues.

"Only a few of us living have been told of the burial site's existence on Tsiwodi, or as you know it, Red Hawk Mountain. The wisdom of this was to leave it unknown and thereby undisturbed. With the threat of mountaintop removal, that wisdom no longer holds." Like Papaw says about words, I guess wisdom needs to be flexible, too.

"Mrs. Whitaker?" I'm surprised at the sound of my own voice breaking the silence.

"Yes, Curley? And you can call me Helen. I already hear the honor in your voice."

"Thank you, ma'am . . . I mean, *Helen*. What does wisdom say now?"

She laughs. "When I hear it, you'll be the first to know." And then she shakes our hands and lets them go.

———

"There's one more thing about *serendipity*, Curley. Something you won't find in any dictionary," Papaw told me when he gave me my word. "You can influence it. You might not be able to make it happen, but you can create the conditions under which it can."

"How's that, Papaw?"

"Stay open to possibility. Be on the lookout for good. And *serendipity* will bless you again and again."

I didn't know what Papaw meant by that when he told me. After meeting Helen? Now I do.

———

Serendipity—*noun*

: the phenomenon of an agreeable and unexpected coincidence, often appearing when searching for something else

T

It's been a crazy week in Wonder Gap, especially after the *Lexington Record* ran that picture of me and Jules in our tree, and no, we were not K-I-S-S-I-N-G. I *cannot* get that dang song out of my head.

We've had all kinds of visitors wanting to sit in Ol' Charley, so Jules and I are only in it for a few hours a day after school. Mrs. C has taken it upon herself to draw up a sit-in schedule and to make sure folks have provisions and such. She also keeps an eye on the progress of the mining road.

Meanwhile, dozens of folks—including many of Mrs. C's environmental friends, Helen's Cherokee friends, and other American Indians from all over Kentucky—have been combing the mountain, searching for anything that might show us where the ancient burial site is. After hundreds of years, Helen explained, it's been covered over by brush and trees. If they find the burial site, we might have a case for trying to preserve it and the mountain with it. Right now, it's our only hope.

Every day, the searchers gather at Ol' Charley and head off up the mountain. They spread out in a line, much like folks do when they're searching for a lost youngster in the backwoods or somebody's granddaddy who's lost his way. It's a little like looking for a needle in a haystack, Papaw says, but we're all hopeful that Ol' Charley has been watching over something special all these years.

Speaking of Papaw, today's the day he's coming home. He's calling it a "visit," which right away makes me think he's not planning to stay. Who the heck visits home, anyway? He says we'll discuss our plans when he gets here, which has me about as nervous as a long-tailed cat in a room full of rocking chairs. I mean, I don't know where our money's going to come from or even where we're going to live for the long haul, now that I've gone and spoken out against Big Coal. Really, I'm speaking out *for* our mountain, but that's a *distinction* (*d* word, last year) Mr. Tiverton apparently doesn't see.

Anyway, Papaw says there's too much happening on Red Hawk Mountain to stay away any longer, and Aunt Gertie has agreed to come back with him. She says it's to help take care of the house, but I know it's to keep an eye on Papaw. Frankly, that's a relief. Even when we've talked on the phone, his pauses make me nervous. I'm afraid he won't get started again.

Today is Saturday, and I thought I'd surprise Papaw with a little welcoming party, which is why I invited Mr. Amons, Jules, Mrs. C, and JD over to the house after Jules and I tidied up. I'll tell you what, she and I were like a couple of worker bees, dusting and sweeping and wiping down cabinets. It's a warm spring day in Wonder Gap, so we threw open all the windows, at least the ones that aren't stuck shut, and Jules picked a bouquet of daffodils for the kitchen table.

"Ma says there's nothing like fresh-cut flowers to remind you of why you're alive," Jules told me. Funny, my ma used to say that, too.

"Anybody home?" Papaw bellows. My heart thump-thumps at the sound of his voice.

"In here, Papaw!" I yell, signaling everybody to hush.

And then, there he is, filling up the doorway.

"Surprise!"

I was planning to act all casual-like and cool when I saw him, you know, in front of my friends. But when he strolls through that doorway and into our kitchen, I can't help myself. Aunt Gertie is standing behind him, waving her hands like a crazy woman, but I ignore her.

"Papaw!" I shout, and leap into him for one of those bear hugs only he can give.

"Whoa there!" He winces. "Still a little tender in the chest."

"Oh, Papaw . . ." I step back, ashamed. "I forgot."

"That's okay, Curley. Come on over here." And with that, he pulls me in real gentle-like. "I sure have missed my boy."

"Awwwww . . ." JD croons behind me.

"Awwwww . . ." Mr. A, Jules, and Mrs. C chime in.

"I see you've called the welcome wagon for us, Curley," Papaw says with his chin resting on my head, "or is this a posse?" Everyone laughs.

After Aunt Gertie has been introduced to our friends and she and Mr. A exchange a longer hug than I feel comfortable watching, she declares, "Well, John . . . do you think it's time to show Curley what we brought down from Cincinnati?"

"As good a time as any," he says.

She comes back from the living room with a shopping bag from Computer World.

"Oh, *maaannn*," JD says. "I like the looks of this."

"What the heck?" Believe me, I can read, and I know what JD *thinks* it is, but I figure there's got to be some kind of trick, like the kind Papaw plays on me at Christmas. But no, I reach for the bag and pull out a seventeen-inch laptop computer.

"Awesome!" Jules and JD shout together.

"Oh my gosh, Papaw. Can I keep it?"

"It's not a puppy. Of course you can keep it."

"But I thought you said you'd never let one of these new-fangled contraptions into the house." I'm pretty sure that at any moment, someone's going to swipe it right out of my hands.

Papaw looks over at Mr. A, who's grinning like all get-out. "Let's just say I've had a change of heart."

"Don't let that ol' cuss fool you. It wasn't that easy." Mr. A hangs an arm around my aunt's shoulders and pulls her closer. "Your Aunt Gertie and I have been prodding him like a stubborn mule to change his ways."

"It was that video you and your friends made, Curley," Papaw says. "That's what did it. If I hung on to those old beliefs I had about computers being no good, I'd be holding you back from what's good for you. I see that now."

"But, Papaw . . . what about the money?" I'm a little embarrassed to bring up the topic in front of my friends, but I have to know.

Papaw looks over at Aunt Gertie, who nods. "Let's just say it was an interfamily loan, but never you mind. You shouldn't be worried about that right now."

He has no idea.

"Come on, Curley, let's get this thing up and running." Papaw slaps me on the back and watches over my shoulder.

"Yeah, Ketchup. Let's take this baby for a spin." JD scoots his chair over closer to me. Jules does the same on the other side. The screen lights up and chimes its welcome. "Too bad you don't have Internet. We could check how many hits we've gotten over the last twenty-four hours."

Ever since his dad took away his electronics, JD's been going through what he calls "withdrawal." I guess computers and such are like a drug to him. Honestly, every waking minute at school when he's not in class, JD's in the computer lab, clicking onto You2CanChangetheWorld.com to check on our video.

"Wait a minute." JD peers into the right-hand corner of the screen. "This says you have service. But . . . How can . . . ?"

JD, Jules, and I look across the kitchen table at Mrs. C, who's covering her mouth, trying to hide a smile.

"Hey, there's more to my life than staging sit-ins," she says.

"We owe Mrs. Cavanaugh a debt of gratitude," Papaw adds, "for helping to get us hooked up. Is that what you call it?" He looks over at Mr. A, who grins and nods.

As I type in the website address for our video, Jules leans over my shoulder, so close her hair tickles my neck. JD is practically drooling over the keyboard.

"Okay, JD. Go ahead." I slide the laptop over. "Don't want you having a conniption fit."

Our count took a jump on Wednesday after our photo hit the papers and has been climbing steadily ever since. Last count at the end of the day on Friday: 8,367. That seemed like a lot to me, but when I yelled, "It's gone viral!" in the middle of the computer lab, JD said, "Settle down, Ketchup. We're not even close."

"H-holy cow," JD stutters as our video pops up on the screen.

All chatter stops. Jules has a death grip on my arm. Papaw, Mr. A, and Aunt Gertie press in, hovering over JD's shoulders, trying to figure out what he's looking at. My own vision blurs as I search the screen for our listing.

And then I see it. *Topless in Wonder Gap*: 957,444 views.

"Whoaaaaaaa!" Mr. A starts the chorus as everyone else joins in.

"This is it!" JD shouts. "It's happening!" He's out of his seat, pacing back and forth, laughing like a madman.

Jules shakes me by the shoulders. "Curley! We did it! We did it!"

The whole thing is so *surreal* (*s* word, fourth grade), I can't even feel what's happening.

JD hits REFRESH. The view count has jumped by several thousand in just a few minutes.

"How does a thing like this happen?" Papaw falls back into a chair, wiping away little beads of sweat with his hand-kerchief. Aunt Gertie races to the sink to pour him some water.

"Somebody tweeted." JD slaps his hand on the table with such force that the daffodils shake. "I guarantee it. Somebody famous saw our video and tweeted."

"Tweeted?" Papaw says. "What the heck is that?"

"It's when people talk about what they're doing or think-ing in very few words," Mr. A tells his friend. "You'd be really bad at it."

Mrs. C, who's been watching the whole scene with this silly grin on her face, suddenly straightens up in her chair like she's all electrified.

"I know who it was," she says.

"Who?" Jules slides around to her ma's side of the table.

"You know that country singer with the real pretty voice, Lena McFadden? The one who was born and raised in Kentucky?" Jules nods and squeezes her ma's arm. "Well, I met her at a protest rally in Frankfort last year. I didn't think she'd remember me, but I sent her the link to your video anyway. I figured it was worth a try."

"Mom, you're a genius." Jules gives her ma such an energetic hug that they almost topple over backward. I'm watching all this and thinking about how the two of them are just like sisters, when I start missing my own ma something fierce. I just wish she could be here to see all this. I think she'd be real proud.

Papaw coughs and I look up in time to see him wince, not like there's a knife in his chest or anything, but like somebody just jabbed him with a finger. He catches me looking at him and says, "It's okay, Curley. Just a little tickle in my throat. I'm fine." He leans across the table and grabs ahold of my hand.

"I'm so proud of you," he says.

That's when I realize that tweets and laptops and videos going viral are exciting and all, but the best thing in my life right now is Papaw being *home*. I glance at my new computer screen and then back at Papaw, who's growing a grin as big as the world.

"All it takes is one, just like you said, Papaw, remember?"

He shakes my hand like he's about to throw down some dice.

"To think I lived to see the day."

———————

Well, it's official. Our video has gone viral. We crossed the one million mark sometime during the cake and ice cream, although by then, JD was the only one paying attention. Don't get me wrong, we were all pretty darn excited. It's just that you can only stare at a computer screen for so long before you start feeling a little touched in the head.

Right around that same time, the phone started ringing. After the first call, Mrs. C answered, keeping what she calls a press calendar. Last count, we've heard from three bloggers, half a dozen reporters, the Associated Press, and three cable news channels—all wanting to do a "piece" on me and Jules and what we're doing to save our mountain.

"It's like you're rock stars," JD said.

One of the cable guys wanted to send somebody down right away to start filming tomorrow, but Mrs. C told them there's nothing much happening in Wonder Gap on a Sunday except for a lot of churchgoing and altar calls. Even Tiverton Coal takes a day off.

So Monday it is. Mrs. C's organizing a press conference after school so that Jules and I don't wear out our voices. We all agree that Helen should be a part of it, too. That's big doings down here in the holler, incidentally. Most days, the rest of the country doesn't pay us any mind.

Jules and I are beside ourselves about what we're going to say. Actually, I'm worried sick about what they might ask me, and she's worried about her hair. We told JD he deserved to be with us. We wouldn't have a video if it weren't for him.

"Guys, you don't understand," he said. "My old man threatened to send me to boarding school if I so much as give you a boost up into Ol' Charley."

So we let him be. Once the media rush was over, everybody went on home except for Jules, who offered to clean up the kitchen while Aunt Gertie, Papaw, and I got settled back in.

It feels strange being home. As good as it is to have Papaw back, I'm already missing Jules. I'll miss watching her feed her ma's chickens, or the "girls," as she calls them. I'll miss seeing her wet hair up in a towel. I'll miss lounging around on the pullout couch, watching Saturday morning cartoons, her in her reindeer pajamas, me in my sweats.

I yank open the top drawer of my dresser to put away my socks, and there's the dream catcher I stole from her back before we knew Red Hawk was in danger. The word for the week was *kleptomaniac*. At the time, I thought a word could make you do things. Now I know the decision to steal was all mine, just like the decision not to 'fess up. As Papaw would say, our words create our world, but we're the creators. *We* decide what kind of world we want to create.

I finger the beads and test the tautness of the web. It has taken a beating, but it's held up pretty well. It's time to give it back . . . but when? A floorboard creaks behind me. I turn, holding the dream catcher behind my back. It's Jules with a fistful of daffodils.

"I picked these for you, Curley." She's talking kind of shy, which catches me off guard. Never in a million years did I expect she'd ever bring me flowers. It's such a girly thing to do. "I thought you could use your own personal 'welcome home.'" She takes a step forward and I think she might hug me, but then she looks down. "Curley, what's that?"

I pull out the dream catcher and think about lying. *I found it tucked inside your couch. I was going to surprise you with it on your birthday, but I guess you've found me out.* But there's no use. Jules can read me like a book. Besides, after all we've been through recently, it doesn't seem right. My hands are shaking. The little black feathers hanging from the hoop spin and sway.

"I took it, Jules."

"Took it? *Why?*"

"I was mad at you for liking JD more than me, I guess. So I took it to see if you'd miss it." I swallow hard. "And you did."

Her pupils are as dark as bullet holes. The daffodils are quivering in her white-knuckled hand. "I thought it was my fault," she says.

"I know. I'm sorry."

"You let me think it was my fault."

"I didn't mean to . . . It's just that . . . I thought you'd hate me if I told you the truth."

"I let you hold me . . ."

"I know, Jules . . . but . . . but you were so . . . *soft* . . ." I try to give her back the dream catcher, but she knocks it to the floor.

"I thought I could trust you, Curley Hines. I thought we could tell each other anything."

She throws the bouquet of daffodils at my feet, and before I can say "I'm sorry" one more time, she's gone.

———————

When I finally drag myself downstairs later that night, the pot of chili Aunt Gertie made for dinner is stone-cold. I light the burner and wait. Papaw's sitting at the kitchen table, staring at my new computer screen. I guess Aunt Gertie taught him a thing or two about computers up in Cincinnati. He doesn't even look up.

"I've got a word for you, Curley. Actually, it's a phrase. It's a perfect fit for everything that's happened today."

Everything? He talks like he knows what's going on in my life, and maybe he used to, but not anymore. Not since his heart attack. Not since I broke Jules's trust and lost my only friend. Just the thought of the dream catcher and the daffodils lying scattered on the floor makes me want to throw this whole pot of chili against the wall. I grip the edges of the stove.

"Please, Papaw . . . no more words," I beg under my breath, but I guess he doesn't hear.

"Aunt Gertie gave me this book to read while I was recovering at her house. It's about the *tipping points* of different kinds of trends, like how certain fashions become wildly popular and what makes a new idea catch on, that kind of thing."

The chili starts to bubble, spitting specks of tomato sauce against the inside edges of the pan. I grab a spoon out of the silverware drawer and slam the drawer shut. "Would you *please* get to the point, Papaw?"

"I'm getting there," Papaw says quietly, like he's trying to turn down my volume. "So I looked up *tipping point* in an online dictionary, since I didn't have access to our Big Book here at home. The phrase *tipping point* comes from the study of physics, but it is also used to explain cultural phenomena— like how your video went viral, for instance." He peers into my face as if he's trying to remember who I am. "I thought you'd like it."

"Yeah, well . . ." I slop some chili into a bowl and eat it standing up.

Papaw clears his throat. "Seems to me, *tipping point* also could be used to describe the point at which someone's life is never going to be the same." He looks at me over his reading glasses. "Like ours, for instance."

My face flares hot, and it's not from Aunt Gertie's chili. I've had it with Papaw's words. "Well, I think it's a miserable excuse for a word, Papaw, not to mention that it's *two* words and you looked it up on the Internet, for crying out loud." A blob of chili dribbles out of my mouth and lands on my shirt. I flick it off.

"Sometimes a word, or in this case a phrase, can be useful for helping us sort things out," Papaw says in that obnoxiously calm voice of his. "Words can put a name to what's happening to us and make it seem more manageable somehow. That doesn't mean we have to like it—what's happening, that is."

I throw my half-eaten bowl of chili in the sink. "And what *is* happening, Papaw? Would you just come out with it?" The weight of what he's holding back hangs heavy in the air.

"You're right, Curley. It's time I cut to the chase." He closes the laptop and studies me for what feels like an eternity. "Regardless of what happens to our mountain," he finally says, "we need to leave Wonder Gap . . . at least for a while."

On some level, this is the news I've been expecting, but it still feels like I'm being sucked into a black hole and the entire kitchen is collapsing around me. Papaw keeps on talking, but his words come into my head all garbled, like I'm underwater—something about closing up the house and moving up to Cincinnati when I get out of school, how he needs to find a way to make money, how Aunt Gertie is remodeling her basement so I can have my own room.

It's the word *room* that breaks over me like a bucket of ice.

"But I've already got my own room." I push by Papaw, knocking over a kitchen chair. "I don't care about your stupid tipping point. I don't care about the money. This is the place my family is buried," I scream. "This is everything I've ever known." And for the first time in my life, I walk out on him.

For the first time in my life, I have the last word.

Tipping Point—*noun*

: a moment in time beyond which a process or situation undergoes a significant and often irrevocable change

About an hour after our fight (well, I guess it was *my* fight), Papaw comes up to my room and apologizes for everything that's happening to us like it's all his fault. As mad as I am about leaving Wonder Gap, I feel even worse for him taking all the blame.

"No, no, no," I tell him, "it's *my* fault. I'm the one who spoke out against Big Coal."

We trade back and forth like that for a while, until Papaw finally puts his hands up like he's stopping traffic. "I guess all this was bound to happen sooner or later, no matter what either of us did," he sighs. "That's the thing about tipping points. They get their start way before you know what's coming, and once you figure it out, it's easier to stop a train."

I thought about Jules and the look on her face before she threw those daffodils at my feet. "Once your life tips, can it ever tip back?" I ask.

"What do you think?" He looks at me with his eyebrows raised, like I already know.

Tipping point is only an hour old and I'm already sick of it.

"Papaw? Would you give me my next word . . . *please?*"

"Funny you should ask," he says. "I was just thinking about how *untenable* this whole situation is. No matter which way we turn, there seems to be no solution."

I groan. "I'm not sure I like that word, either, Papaw."

He tilts his head forward and gives me one of those "get with it" looks.

"I know . . . The word isn't the problem," I say in a sing-songy voice. "I just wish it could get us out of it."

I go to bed thinking about how *untenable* my life has become, particularly relating to Jules. Stealing the dream catcher was bad enough, but keeping the truth from her was *untenable*. I realize that now and there's no excuse. I go to bed wrestling with these thought demons, as Papaw would call them, and work up an awful sweat. Halfway through the night, I open a window. A cool breeze carries the scent of lilac and pine. It gentles around me like one of Mama's lullabies.

The sun is shining and that same breeze is blowing as Jules and I walk up Red Hawk Mountain. I'm itching to take

215

her hand, but I reach in my pocket for old Gloria instead. I'm playing "She'll Be Coming 'Round the Mountain" when out of nowhere comes this humongous KABOOM! Boulders and rock fragments are flying all around us, and the ground beneath our feet starts to break apart. Old Gloria falls into a gaping crevice as I grab for Jules's hand and pull her toward me, but she beats on my arm, screaming, "Let go, Curley Hines! I don't trust you! Let me go!"

But I can't let her go because our hands have become fused from the heat of the explosion and we're stuck on this tiny island of earth sliding down the mountain at a frightening speed, and here comes Ol' Charley right behind us, running on his roots.

We finally land next to my family's headstones in the grassy plateau above our house. Ol' Charley plops himself down next to us, plunging his root-legs into the ground. At first I think we're all safe until a swarm of mosquitoes the size of crows flies out of my daddy's grave, buzzing and hovering around us, ready to strike.

"Curley!" Jules screams, trying to swat them away with her free hand. "Do something!" But I'm frozen to my family's plot, unable to move.

I wake to the sound of pebbles hitting the side of the

house and Jules yelling, "Curley!" But the sun is barely up and those mosquitoes are still buzzing. Am I dreaming? I stumble to the window. Jules is looking up at me, pleading. Her face tells it all.

"It's Ol' Charley, Curley! They're cutting him down!"

She takes off at a run back in the direction of the chain saws. *But it's Sunday*, I say to myself as I pull a pair of jeans on over the T-shirt I wore to bed, slip into my hiking boots, and sail down the stairs two at a time. *I thought we were safe.*

Papaw sticks his head out of his bedroom door. "What's all the ruckus, Curley?"

"Ol' Charley, Papaw. I've got to help Jules."

I take the path at a full run, but by the time I get there, it's obvious I'm too late. Chunks of wood are strewn everywhere. Dozens of branches, like so many body parts, lie scattered on the ground around Ol' Charley, his trunk already cut to half its original height. I recognize our special branch, pushed to the side like some cast-off piece of garbage.

One of Mr. Tiverton's goons wields a gigantic chain saw, making V-shaped slashes just above the hollow part where Jules and I used to hide, while another worker tries to hold Jules back as she struggles to break free. I'm just about to yell at him to let her go when she slips from his grasp and rushes at the foreman, who shuts down his saw as soon as he sees her coming.

I'm reminded once again of screaming banshees, and I don't know which sounds worse, the high-pitched whine of a chain saw grinding through three-hundred-year-old wood, or the desperation of my best friend's screams.

"What the—?" the man yells as he turns around. Jules is yanking on his orange vest, like one of those pesky little dogs nipping at an intruder's heels. The whole scene has me frozen in place, that and seeing how Ol' Charley's life has been chipped away, limb by ancient limb.

"Sorry, bud." The other worker pulls Jules away, trying to stay clear of her kicking feet. "She's a slippery one," he says as the foreman pulls the cord on the chain saw and makes one last cut.

"Jules!" I scream as she yanks herself free once again, tripping over a log and falling into a pile of sawdust.

I rush in to help her—there's no telling which way Ol' Charley's going to fall or when—but just like in my dream, she doesn't want my help. She pushes me away and struggles to stand.

"Let me go, Curley. We've got to stop him!" She springs

for the man as he turns off the saw. *Does she not understand that his job is already done?* I wonder in desperation.

"Are you out of your ever-loving mind?" the foreman screams. "This tree could fall at any minute!" He grabs Jules by the arm and starts dragging her up the path.

That's when it breaks. My heart. My rage. Split wide open down the middle of me.

"Let go of her *now*, you stupid jerk!"

I throw myself at his back, knocking the three of us down onto the soft, leaf-covered ground. Jules rolls away, but I'm still on top of him. He covers his head as I beat on him with my fists, spewing all the foul words Papaw told me never to say.

"What have you done?" I scream, foaming at the mouth like a rabid dog. "I want Ol' Charley back. Put. Him. *Back*." Off to the side, I hear Jules sobbing.

My arms are beginning to feel as limp as noodles, when I feel two strong hands grab ahold of my shoulders and pull me up. At first I think it must be the other worker and I'm ready to let another fist fly, but then I see it's Papaw. Jules is clinging to Mrs. C.

"There, there, son." Papaw strokes the top of my head as I sink into him. "This is a terrible thing."

We're standing like that when Mr. Tiverton himself emerges from the woods. He looks around, refusing to acknowledge any of us.

"Why isn't this tree *down*?" he shouts at his men.

"We've had a little trouble with the locals," the foreman mutters, brushing leaves and sawdust off his jeans.

"You haven't seen anything yet," Papaw says under his breath.

"What's that, Mr. Weaver?" Mr. Tiverton takes a step toward us.

"I said, you haven't *begun* to see the trouble we're about to cause."

"I'm sorry to hear that, John . . . mostly for you and your grandson here."

"Let's get one thing perfectly clear, *Jim*. Curley and I have made our choice, and we're not sorry at all." Papaw tightens his arm around me, and I've never been prouder.

"Well, I think I better warn you, then," Mr. Tiverton replies. "We'll be torching these hills by the end of the week to get this lease ready for mining." Jules lunges like she's going to jump him, but her mother holds her back.

Mr. Tiverton shakes his head and studies the ground, as though he's lost something valuable in all those wood chips and sawdust. "Look. I know you kids aren't very happy with me right now, but we need to move forward on this lease. We'll save what we can, but most of these trees will have to go."

CRACK!

"Stand clear!" the foreman yells.

Ol' Charley groans, teeters, and falls, slowly, like an old man slumping to the ground. All that remains is his hollow part, open to the sky.

Someone lets out a wail that sounds more like a war cry. I can't tell if it's Jules or if it's me, our despair seems so inseparable.

Papaw whispers into my ear, *"Go!"* and gives me a nudge.

The next thing I know, Jules and I are in each other's arms.

———

Untenable—*adjective*

: not capable of being maintained or supported; not defensible; as an untenable doctrine; untenable ground in argument

We've agreed to meet Helen by Ol' Charley at the crack of dawn, that is, at the time the sun would normally rise if there wasn't a mountain in the way. On this side of the Appalachians, dawn doesn't actually "crack." It's more like a slow roll through mist and shadow. By the time the sun appears in all of its roundness, the morning will be half-gone.

Papaw and I pour a thermos of steaming hot coffee and go by the Cavanaughs', where Jules and her ma come out to join us. Chickadees, cardinals, and mockingbirds are beginning to stir within the fog-shrouded canopy. Jules shuffles past Papaw to walk by my side and slides a hand in my jacket pocket for warmth. We don't say a word.

Papaw's always talking about "life's greatest mysteries." Well, one of those mysteries happened yesterday between me and Jules, when Ol' Charley fell and left us empty, and then all that hugging and holding made us all of a sudden full.

And in case you think we were cheating on JD, we never kissed. We never even held hands. We did hold on to each other for the longest time, crying over Ol' Charley. For the rest of the day, we were inseparable, like how we were back in the olden days before JD, only different.

You can't imagine what a relief it is after the dream catcher incident to know we're still friends. Sometimes it takes a great sadness, Papaw says, to remind you of what really matters.

Now that it's May and all the leaves are out, it's harder to see up the mountain or even down the path, so when we come around the bend to the place where Ol' Charley used to stand, we are caught completely off guard. We expected to see Helen, but standing with her in a circle around a section of Ol' Charley's trunk are over a dozen folks in what look like ceremonial regalia—the women in long silk dresses with bands of diamonds circling their skirts, the men in colorful ribbon shirts, jeans, and moccasins. It takes me a minute to recognize Sheriff Whitaker out of uniform. He nods and smiles sadly at us. His ma is leaning over a rock, preparing something. He bends down to whisper to her, and her face lights up when she sees us.

"Ah . . . our friends!" Helen beckons. She's wearing a long white dress with bands of turquoise and gold. Around her waist is a beaded belt with hummingbirds near the tasseled ends. "We are so glad you've come."

The circle opens to make room for us. Jules stands beside me and links her arm through mine, something she has never done. I look around the circle. This must be what everyone else is doing, but no. She must be cold, I tell myself. She just wants to get warm.

An early morning mist hangs in sheets around the open space created by the mining road. Ol' Charley's many branches and sections of trunk are stacked outside the circle. Our favorite branch, the one we used to sit on, is lying off on its own nearby.

Helen leans into her son as he lights a stick of what looks like tightly bound grass over the cup of an empty shell. Once lit, the end of the stick smokes and glows like the tobacco in one of Papaw's pipes. It smells like Thanksgiving. Helen approaches us, smiling. Beginning with Papaw, she waves her hand over the stick and bathes each one of us in smoke from head to toe. "This is called smudging, my friends. It's what we do to clear away negativity before we enter into anything sacred."

You came to the right people, I think as I look down at the sea of sawdust that used to be Ol' Charley covering the ground at our feet.

Helen returns to her original spot. I could have sworn she was no higher than a fence post, but here among her people, she stands straight and tall. As she stretches out her arms to encompass the circle, her long, fringed shawl opens wide behind her like a white bird unfolding its wings. She is old and she is beautiful, a *venerable* presence, as Papaw would say—in fact, *did* say last night when he gave me my new word. He said I'd already lived out a year's worth of *untenable* in a single day.

Helen addresses the circle. "We are here to honor the life of this beautiful tree that has given so much to our people. We do this by offering the gift of tobacco and, of course, our prayers."

She draws a handful of tobacco out of a leather pouch. Raising her cupped hand to the sky, she turns and offers blessings to each of the four directions, and then, facing into the circle, she adds three more—above, below, and within. At least, I think she means "within," since she's tapping her fist gently over her heart. I never thought about "within" as being a direction, but now that I think about it, there are days when so much is going on inside me, that's the only direction I see.

After acknowledging the seven directions, Helen lets the tobacco fall through her fist, drawing a perfect circle on Ol'

Charley's trunk. Each member of the gathering then steps forward to honor Ol' Charley with their gift of tobacco while speaking prayers in their native language. Many of the words Papaw gives me have their origins in the fifteenth or sixteenth centuries, and I've always thought *they* were old. But these words? These *sounds* forming somewhere beneath their tongues? They feel as old as the mountains.

After everyone but the four of us has said their prayers, Helen and her son walk around the circle to where we stand, offering each of us a handful of tobacco from a leather pouch so that we, too, can pay our respects.

Papaw walks up to Ol' Charley and scatters his tobacco first. "Thank you, Old One," he says, "for watching over our mountain."

When it's her turn, Mrs. C puts a hand on Ol' Charley and bows her head. "Thank you for protecting our children," she prays, "and for never letting them fall."

As for me, I sprinkle my tobacco slowly. I'm so full of memories and sadness, all I can do is stand there, feeling my heart thump. I just can't find the words. Finally, I give up and trudge back to Papaw's side.

And then there's Jules.

Jules marches right up to Ol' Charley, all business—like she's going to throw that tobacco down and be done with it—but then she falls to her knees, crying. I mean, the sound of her sobbing echoes clear down the holler. I want to run over and make her feel better, but all the solemn faces around the circle hold me back. And then it hits me, the thing that Helen and her friends seem to know:

Jules is praying, too. Her tears are her prayers.

After the longest time, Jules picks herself up and heads back to us, wiping her eyes on her jacket sleeve. I'm all set to let her link her arm in mine again, but she leans into her ma instead.

Helen raises her face to the sky as the rest of the circle takes hands. *"Hoyana osda Unetlana wado,"* she begins. "We thank You, Creator, for the support Ol' Charley has offered these two young people, Curley and Jules, and we ask that You continue to bless them. May You continue to bless *all* of us and our ancestors, too, as You show us the way to our ancient burial site, our sacred ground. Show us how to protect it, so that we may teach future generations to honor the old ways."

When she's finished, everyone in the circle says, *"Aho,"* which feels a lot like "amen." Papaw and I aren't Sunday-go-to-meeting people, but this whole morning has felt way holier than any altar call I ever witnessed at Anna Ludlow's church on the rare occasions she's invited me.

Helen picks up her cane and leans against it as she looks across the circle at me, Papaw, Jules, and Mrs. C. "Thank you for coming, my friends. This occasion would not have been the same without you. We think of you as our tree's guardians and are grateful for your protection."

"But . . ." I start to object, feeling guilty all over again about letting Ol' Charley down.

She raises a hand. "There was nothing you could do to stop this. The end of this life was ordained." She looks lovingly at the place Ol' Charley used to stand. "This tree has served its purpose. It has protected our mountain for hundreds of years. Now it's our turn."

"Aho," a few of her people say.

"Does that mean you've found the burial site?" Jules asks in a quiet voice, softened even more by the morning mist.

A tall man with a long black braid down his back steps into the circle and speaks. "We have found indications of a burial mound at the very top of the mountain," he says. "There are archeologists in Wonder Gap right now, beginning a preliminary investigation."

Jules and I look at each other in amazement. Could it really be?

"Tiverton's planning to torch all the trees on top of the mountain," Papaw announces to the gathering. "He's threatened to start sometime this week."

The man shakes his head. "We were afraid of that. Hopefully, the archeologists will find something soon."

"And having public opinion on our side should help," Helen adds, looking over Ol' Charley at Jules and me.

I'm about to remind her about the press conference this afternoon, when we hear a series of doors slamming along the county road several hundred yards away. It's impossible to see who our visitors might be, given the thick undergrowth of the woods. I glance down at Papaw's oversized wristwatch and see that it's not yet 8:00 a.m.—too early for Tiverton's men, but then, I thought they didn't work on Sundays, either.

"Before we're joined by the others, whoever they may be," Helen proceeds calmly, "we are here today, not only to honor this tree, but to move it—at least in part. We may not have been able to prevent Ol' Charley's demise, but we can certainly determine a resting place where the tree as a whole can be remembered. Any idea where that might be?" She's speaking to Jules and me now.

I gaze at the section of trunk Helen is proposing to move, and I want to say, *That's not Ol' Charley.* But then, if what Mr. A says about DNA is true, the whole is encoded in every part. I think of our family cemetery up on the grassy plateau above our house. Maybe my dream was giving me a premonition of where Ol' Charley's memorial is supposed to be.

I look over at Jules. She grips my arm and leans in close to my ear. "By your mama and little Zeb, Curley . . . and your daddy, too," she whispers. "That would make a real nice place for us to sit."

She sees us together. Blood rushes to my face.

Speechless, I look over at Helen and nod in the direction toward home.

"Curley." Jules points. A caravan of television news vans is now parked along the mining road. Several camera operators are already strapping on their gear, accompanied by folks who look like reporters.

"And so it begins," Papaw says.

Helen stares down the road at the cameras as the others wait for direction. "We do not usually allow the photographing of sacred ceremonies, but in this case, we must make an exception." She motions for her people to gather along Ol' Charley's trunk—the part we have just blessed. For such a small, seemingly frail woman, she commands a heap of respect. She nods. They lift.

"Come, you two." She extends her hand up the path toward our property. "Show us the way." Helen, Papaw, and Mrs. C drop in behind us, followed by the rest of the group carrying Ol' Charley.

I try to keep my mind focused on the sacredness of the procession—but I can't help but wonder if those cameras are getting any of this on film. Maybe it's all those reality shows Jules and I watched while Papaw was gone, but I've got to believe this could get us the kind of publicity Helen is hoping for.

Once we make the climb to the plateau, I show Helen the area I have in mind, several yards from my family's graves. Her people set Ol' Charley down but continue to stand around like they're waiting for further instructions.

I feel a sudden rush of sadness seeing Ol' Charley stripped of his branches and out of the woods like this. Jules and I will never again crawl into his hollow trunk to get away from it all. I'll never lift her onto our branch again, follow her up, and dillydally the day away. Lord knows I could use some dillydallying right about now.

And yet, here he is. Helen's ceremony has helped me see we still have him in a way. It's like Jules and I have our own church now, up here with my kin. The Church of Ol' Charley.

"How do you want us to place him?" Helen asks me gently, waking me from my thoughts. "When you sit on Ol' Charley, which way do you want to look?"

I think about the seven directions. Do I want to face east up the mountain, or west toward home? After all, both places are sacred.

"That way," I say, pointing north. Helen nods and motions for her people to set Ol' Charley down in the tall grass, just so.

Jules searches in the direction I pointed, as if she's wondering what kind of sacred site I have in mind, or maybe if I've lost my mind.

"Why north, Curley?"

I pull up a long stalk of grass and nod in the direction of her home.

"Because that's where you are."

Venerable—*adjective*

1 : capable of being venerated; worthy of veneration

or reverence; deserving of honor and respect; generally implying an advanced age

2 : rendered sacred by religious or other associations; that should be regarded with awe and treated with reverence; as, the venerable walls of a temple or a church

Lunch period is the first chance Jules and I get to see JD and fill him in on everything that's happened in the last forty-eight hours since we saw him. Turns out, he already knew about a lot of it. I guess you could say he has an inside source.

"Yeah, my old man was telling me about knocking down your tree at dinner the other night. He said you guys created quite the scene." He puts an arm around Jules, who's sitting next to him at the lunch table, and gives her a little squeeze. He looks across the table at me. "I love a girl who's got swag, don't you?"

If I didn't know about *rhetorical* questions (*r* word, fifth grade), I'd be tempted to answer that, but watching Jules's reaction is a lot more interesting. What JD might think is a smile is most definitely a wince.

"That tree that your father 'knocked down' was three hundred years old—sacred to the Cherokee and sacred to *me*!"

She shrugs his arm off her shoulder. "And that 'swag,' as you call it, came from losing one of the most important parts of my childhood. *Our* childhood—Curley's and mine." She scowls at me across the table, like it's my fault, too.

"Hey, Jules, I wasn't dissing you, honest." JD shoots me this pleading look.

"Yeah, Jules. JD was trying to compliment you, you know; he loves that you're a fighter."

"Yeah, that's right." JD brightens. "You know there's nothing I'd rather see than somebody getting the best of my old man." JD leans over to look up into Jules's face, all puppy-dog-like. "I'm proud of you."

Jules starts packing up her lunch tray like she's leaving on vacation. Knife and fork here, milk carton there, wadded napkin tossed into her uneaten beef stew. "For your information, James David Tiverton III, we did not get the best of your father. He cut Ol' Charley *down*." She slams the tray on the table for effect, picks it up again, and is gone.

"What the . . . ?"

Poor guy has no idea what just happened, and I want to make him feel better, honest I do. But nothing I can say could possibly change the way he looks at the world . . . or Jules.

"Sorry, JD," I say. "I think she just wanted to hear that you're sorry about her tree."

———————

Mrs. C picks Jules and me up at school at the end of the day to drive us back to my house for our press conference. She tries to prepare us for what to expect. Now that our video has gone viral, it seems that some of our viewers have taken me up on my invitation to visit Wonder Gap.

"Your fan base has arrived by the *droves*," Mrs. C says. "They're all looking for Ol' Charley, of course, and they get awful mad when they find out what happened to him. Three people from Ohio even lay down in front of the bulldozer before it got to Ol' Charley's stump and wouldn't let it pass. Tiverton's men finally had to shut down operations altogether, at least for today."

Jules and I are excited about all that, of course, and grateful for the support, but the mention of "droves" of people invading our holler has both of us on edge. That, plus the thought of all of those cameras staring us down, and we've got a serious case of the willies.

"My stomach's got butterflies," Jules says, chewing on a chunk of her hair.

"Mine has squirrels," I say, and she laughs. "I'm serious, Jules. It feels like they're tumbling all over each other."

It's not as if we haven't thought about what we're doing. Mr. Amons met with us during study hall to go over the questions the press threw out at us earlier today as we left for school and didn't have time to answer. When we got to the question "What's the nature of your relationship?" Jules and I looked at each other, waiting for the other to answer first.

"Well?" Mr. A waited expectantly. "This one should be easy."

"Friends," I finally said.

"Right . . . friends," Jules echoed.

Mr. A cocked his head to the side for a second. "And so . . . it would seem that the simple answer to 'Are you dating?' would be . . . ?"

"No," we both answered simultaneously.

"Okay, then," he said, running his hand over his bald spot, "as long as you're both on the same page. You can always answer, 'No comment,' but I wouldn't advise it. They'll come at you like a school of piranhas." I found this about as reassuring as when Mrs. C told me that Papaw was okay but was on his way to the hospital in a helicopter.

In addition to prepping us, Mr. A has offered to come to the press conference and hand out fact sheets about mountaintop removal. He said he thinks it's important that folks hear about the "bigger picture."

"One of these days, Curley, I think you're going to find that saving your mountain isn't enough."

"That's just fine, Mr. A, but until that day comes, saving Red Hawk is about all I've got the stomach for." When I consider what this fight has already meant to me and Papaw, I hate to think what an entire mountain range would cost.

Mrs. C eases her Jeep through the throngs of people waving and cheering at us on both sides of my driveway and, of course, we wave back. They're as crazy excited as a crowd at a homecoming football game. As a kid who never made the cut into varsity anything, I never thought I'd get to feel this way.

Some folks are waving signs that read, SAVE RED HAWK MOUNTAIN and JUST SAY NO TO COAL. One sign even says, A TOPLESS MOUNTAIN IS AN OXYMORON, which, I don't mind telling you, adds to the thrill.

"Look, Curley, they quoted you!" Jules says, as if reading my mind.

Mrs. C pulls into the side yard away from the crowd that's forming around the front porch, where a microphone stand has been set up above the steps. We jump out of the Jeep and rush through the back door into the kitchen, where Papaw and Aunt Gertie are waiting for us with fresh-baked cookies and milk.

"Oh, Papaw, I don't know if I'm ready for this," I say, nibbling around the edges of an oatmeal raisin cookie.

"Me neither," says Jules. She's ignored the cookies altogether, which isn't like her at all. She's sitting next to me at the kitchen table and kicking my chair with her foot. I don't think she even knows she's doing it.

"There are only two things you need to remember," Papaw says, lighting his pipe. "Be yourselves." How many times have I heard *that* one?

"And?"

"And remember what you stand for."

No sooner does he say that than I start thinking about Tiverton Coal torching trees and blowing up Red Hawk, and I'm itching to talk. Papaw blows a stream of smoke out the side of his mouth and leans in closer to me. I can smell the woodsy scent of his breath.

"All the answers you need are inside you, Curley. You know that. But . . . if for some reason you get stuck, don't be afraid to wonder. Wonder aloud."

I'm always on the lookout for my next word, but until a few weeks ago, I've only needed to pay attention on Sundays. These days, they're coming at me every which way like a field full of fillies.

"That's the next word, isn't it, Papaw? *Wonder*?"

Papaw chuckles. "Well, now that you mention it, I guess *wonder* is your next word. It makes sense, doesn't it, considering where we come from?" He slaps me on the back. "Feel free to use it or not, son, but I will say this: *Wonder* has a way of opening folks up."

"Come on, Curley. Let's do this thing." Jules pulls me out of my chair. Her cheeks are flushed, and I wonder if I'll ever get to stick my finger in that dang dimple of hers.

"Curley?" she says. Her hand waits in the air.

"Oh, right," I say, giving her a high five, perfectly placed, I might add.

"For our mountain," she says.

"For our mountain!" Aunt Gertie, Papaw, and Mrs. C repeat as they gently nudge us out the door.

The crowd erupts as soon as we walk onto the porch, hundreds of them, screaming and cheering and shaking signs. The only thing I've experienced that comes close to this feeling is that UK Wildcat basketball game Papaw took me to last winter up in Lexington. As soon as the team took the floor, the crowd went wild—hooting and hollering something awful. So this is kind of like that, only without the indoor fireworks, if you can imagine. There is also a row of cameras, some with enormous lenses, lined up in front of the porch, and a dozen or so reporters holding microphones.

As planned, Mrs. C speaks to the crowd first, giving them some background on Tiverton Coal and what the company is planning on doing to our mountain. Honestly, I don't hear much of it since I'm so busy searching the crowd for anyone I might know. Papaw says it's a good idea to pick out somebody and talk to that one person. That's part of his "all it takes is one" rule. That way you don't get to feeling overwhelmed.

Thankfully, I find a number of familiar faces to choose from. Mr. A's here, of course, milling through the crowd, passing out flyers. And there are the Donnelly sisters, Ida and Rosa May. They look kind of closed in and anxious, what with all the jumping and hollering going on around them. Anna Ludlow and her ma are standing at the edge of the crowd over by Ma's peonies. Mrs. Ludlow has her head wrapped in a blue-and-white-checkered scarf. Anna doesn't talk about it much, but I know Mrs. C's been driving Mrs. Ludlow to the hospital for chemo. Mrs. C says she's got a rare form of leukemia caused by their tainted drinking water, another deadly effect of mountaintop removal, or so Mrs. C says.

I'm wondering how hard the whole thing must be for Anna, when I notice Gordy the dozer guy standing way in the back with an older man in a Harley jacket, both of them grinning like they're at some kind of motorcycle rally. I bet the older guy is his pa. Gordy catches my eye and tips his cap.

Sheriff Whitaker and several of his deputies are stationed on either side of the porch, I guess to make sure we don't start a riot or anything. They all look pretty happy. This kind of radical activity doesn't come through Wonder Gap very often. I don't see Sheriff Whitaker's ma, though. I could really use Helen's venerable presence right about now.

I don't know how I could have missed him, but I see Jules break into a smile and wave at JD standing smack-dab in the middle of everything, right behind the line of reporters and cameras. I guess at some point today, they must have made up. I'm surprised to see him here in enemy territory, though. Mr. A must have given him a ride. If Mr. Tiverton finds out he's here, there'll be hell to pay.

JD gives Jules and me a thumbs-up. We give it right back.

I still haven't decided on that one person I'm going to talk to, when all of a sudden, Mrs. C is introducing us. On the way home from school, Jules and I decided that I would be the main speaker, although she's promised to jump right in if she thinks of something to say, or if I go blank. She said, "Don't worry, Curley. I've got your back," which is something JD would say, but I didn't mind. It sounded pretty good to me.

"Hi, y'all!" I shout. My voice echoes through the holler, and I remember Aunt Gertie warning me to let the mike do the work. "Welcome to Wonder Gap!" Jules and I wave. More applause. Folks are waving back.

As I wait for everyone to settle down, I notice this guy standing behind JD with his arms crossed tight over his chest. He has this grim look on his face, and I wonder if he's one of Mr. Tiverton's men come to spy on the proceedings. But no, I think he's just unhappy.

He's the one.

"Jules and I are glad you're here," I begin, looking right at him. His gaze is so intense that I already need a break from it. "But if you don't mind my saying, all y'all are looking the wrong way." It's funny to see everybody look around, the man included, wondering what the heck I'm talking about.

"A really good friend of mine once said that Red Hawk isn't just *my* mountain, it's *our* mountain." JD's grinning from ear to ear. "At the time, he meant it was mine and Jules's. Recently, I discovered that the Cherokee also treasure it. And now that you are here, it's your mountain, too. So go ahead, turn around and take a nice long look."

Most everyone does just that, which I appreciate. It's that time of day when the trees at the top of the mountain are bathed in golden light from a low-hanging sun. We couldn't have asked for a more spectacular view.

"This is what Jules and I used to do when we sat up in Ol' Charley. We'd sit there and stare at our mountain and wonder about it, like how it got there and how could anything be so beautiful. We didn't need to talk. It's like the mountain did our talking for us."

Some people continue to gaze. Others, like the man, turn back to listen. He seems suspicious of me, like he thinks I'm playing some kind of trick.

"A mountain like Red Hawk inspires us to wonder," I continue. "Take away the mountain and our wonder is gone."

Right now, I'm wondering about that man.

"Who are you?" I say with more edge to my voice than I'd like. Jules whips her head around and stares at me, like I've lost my mind. A familiar look.

"Why are you here?" I pause for a moment, as if expecting an answer.

"Perhaps you work for a coal company, and you think your life depends on coal. If that's true, I respect that. I used to think *my* life depended on coal, too." I notice Gordy the dozer guy nodding along with a few other folks.

"But then I realized that the life I was holding on to on account of coal wasn't a life I wanted to live, especially if it meant living without my mountain."

I hear a few whistles and a catcall or two. JD shouts, "Tell it, Curley!"

"You see . . ." I listen to the echo of my voice rolling through the holler, and I feel my mind go blank. I know I had something really important to say, but it just took off, like the train left the station without me. "You see . . ." Any second now, I'm expecting it to come on back.

Someone shouts: "We love you, Curley Hines!" A tall, blond-haired girl toward the back of the crowd is jumping up and down with three of her girlfriends. Now I'm wondering where *they* came from, but, thankfully, not out loud like Papaw wanted me to do.

Jules rolls her eyes at me and steps up to the mike. "I think what Curley's trying to say . . ." She waits for the cheering section in the back to settle down and then begins again.

"I think what we *both* want you to know . . ." Her voice catches like a sob is stuck at the back of her throat, but she pushes through it. "Oh, gosh . . . *We miss our tree.*"

A full kind of quiet settles on the crowd. I find myself clearing my throat even though Jules is the one talking. *That girl.* She has a way of cutting to the chase, as Papaw would say, with just a few thin words.

"As many of you know, Tiverton Coal cut Ol' Charley down yesterday to make way for a mining road." Jules waits for the booing to stop. "But as much as Curley and I are going to miss sitting up in Ol' Charley, we would miss our mountain a whole lot more. It's kind of like Curley was saying. Around these parts, life without a mountain to wonder on is no life at all."

Well, that does it. Watching her talk from her heart like that makes mine bust wide open, and before I know it, I'm planting a kiss on her cheek in the vicinity of that dimple, right in front of God, our neighbors, Lexington News at 6, and, well, *everybody*.

Jules pulls back a few inches from my face and stares at me. I expect her to give me that "have you lost your ever-lovin' mind" look, but she's full-out blushing instead. She reaches for my arm to steady herself.

"I'm sorry, Jules," I whisper. "I don't know what came over me."

I guess the mike picks up my words, because I hear a voice from the crowd shout, "I do!"

Oh, Lord, it's JD.

People are starting to laugh, and I'm not sure if it's a "laughing at" or a "laughing with." What must JD be thinking? His own best friend kissing his girl—in front of a national audience. What was *I* thinking?

That's just it. I wasn't.

But JD's not storming the porch, ready to tear my guts out. No. He's applauding along with everyone else. How can that possibly be?

And Jules. She's smiling, too. Shy, but smiling. Could it be that instead of stepping into something excremental this time, I actually stepped into something *fine*?

Right when I have no idea what to say next, I hear Mr. A's booming voice start to chant, "Save our mountain! Save our mountain!" and I wonder if he knows he's also saving my goat. He's soon joined by everyone around him, including the man I've been addressing at the center of the crowd, who is now pumping his fist in the air to punctuate every phrase.

"Okay, you two." Mrs. C covers the mike to talk to us while the crowd continues to chant. "I think it's time to take some questions from the press—if you think you're up for it."

"Sure," Jules says.

Bring 'em on, I want to shout, but I nod instead. Actually, I'm relieved to be fielding questions right about now. At least that's something we've rehearsed.

What I'm not ready for is what happens next with Jules. Like . . . what do I do with her hand that's still holding my arm? Should I take it in mine? I'd like to. And what do I do now that I've kissed her? Should I kiss her again? And when? Certainly not here. And dang, if they aren't asking us about our relationship, right off the bat. What should I say now? Has it changed? Are we still friends?

"No comment," says Jules, smiling coyly at the press, setting off that feeding frenzy Mr. A warned us about.

"No comment," I add, catching the eye of our science teacher laughing his head off.

That's when I also notice Helen winding her way through the crowd, followed by a short, heavyset gentleman in a white shirt and a dark brown suit, carrying a piece of paper in his hand.

I've never been so glad to see someone in all my life.

"Greetings from the Cherokee," Helen begins as she steps up to the microphone. "We bring great news." She looks straight down at the lineup of reporters and cameramen to make sure she has their attention. "We have confirmed the location of an ancient Cherokee burial site on Red Hawk Mountain."

You can almost feel the whole crowd catch its breath. Loud murmurs ripple through the audience. Jules still hasn't let go of my arm, and now she's tugging on it like she's milking a cow, not that I'm complaining.

"And there's more to the site than we thought." Helen turns around and winks at us. "We didn't just discover one burial mound, but an entire system of mounds covering a large section of the mountaintop. In addition to this discovery, we've also discovered *another* site—ancient petroglyphs on a rock outcropping at the base of the mountain buried under trees and brush. The petroglyphs tell the story of ancient Cherokee life here in the mountains of Kentucky. There is no doubt in any of our minds that this mountain, Tsiwodi, was considered a sacred mountain by our ancestors going back to the beginning of time.

"Some folks would like to believe that our people only used Kentucky as a hunting ground—that we were just passing through. This discovery puts that myth to rest for good."

Jules's eyes look like they're about to bug right out of their sockets, and I'm sure mine do, too. Helen hands the microphone over to the man standing next to her, introducing him as Justin Henry, a Cherokee tribal lawyer.

"Not only have the experts found human remains," he begins, "they have also found Cherokee artifacts dating back two thousand years, complete with symbols of the Bird Clan. This discovery is exciting to the Cherokee—as it should be to *all* of us—because it connects the people of the present with the people of the past. Because of this, the archeologists are designating this site as one with 'national historic significance.'"

I'm noticing a lot of puzzled faces when Mr. Henry quickly adds, "That may sound like a mouthful, my friends, but it has led to *this*." And he holds the piece of paper above his head.

"This is a copy of a federal injunction I've just delivered to Tiverton Coal. It orders them to halt their mining operation here on Red Hawk Mountain."

Cheers erupt. Jules and I are holding on to each other's arms at the elbows, jumping up and down . . . until Mr. Henry raises his hand again.

"Unfortunately, this order is only effective until the federal court rules on whether or not the site should be preserved. That could take a while. A lot depends on what more the archeologists find . . . and a lot also depends on *you*."

Ever since Tiverton Coal has been threatening to blow up Red Hawk Mountain, I've had a fire in my gut to save it. Now that I've met Helen and stood in a circle with her and her friends? That fire has flared into a raging bonfire at the thought of their sacred burial grounds getting all torn up. There's so much more to lose.

Helen hands Mr. Henry a clipboard.

"This is a petition to the federal court to rule in favor of preservation," Mr. Henry continues. "There's power in numbers, and there seems to be a whole lot of folks who have heard about our mountain recently . . . and they *care*." He smiles at me and Jules. "This petition could be the very thing that not only saves our sacred sites, but saves Red Hawk Mountain for good."

The crowd is applauding like crazy now. Mr. Henry hands the petition down to Mr. A, who immediately signs it and starts passing it around. JD is giving Jules and me another thumbs-up. I return it, wishing he could be up here with us.

"My friends," Mr. Henry continues once the applause has died down. "There is much to celebrate here, *but* . . . we can't afford to celebrate for long. Please hear me. Although we're cautiously optimistic, we need everyone to remain vigilant of the mountain until the process is complete. Orders such as the one I hold in my hand can sometimes be ignored by those who would just as soon pay a fine than compromise their bottom line."

I don't know about the rest of the folks, but those of us who come from the mountains know all too well that what he says is true, and there's a whole lot of boo-hissing going on. Mr. Henry steps back from the microphone, inviting Helen forward again. Everyone hushes to hear her final words.

"What started as a young man's plea to save his mountain has now become so much more. That, my friends, is the power of a single voice." She holds up one finger in the air.

"Imagine the power of many." She raises both arms to encompass the crowd, letting her invitation hang in the air.

"These two young people here beside me—Curley and Jules—have cast a vision for Red Hawk Mountain," she says, almost in a whisper. "And it's up to all of us to keep that vision alive."

"Aho," Jules and I both say, laughing shyly at each other. It certainly feels like the perfect time for an "amen." I sure do hope the Creator knows Jules and I could use some help watching over our mountain right now, especially since I might not be around to watch it with her.

Fortunately, the press is now focused on Helen and her lawyer friend, because I'm in no shape to be "on" anymore. I know that sounds strange, what with the good news we just heard and all, but the thought of leaving Wonder Gap has sent me sliding. I feel like I'm sinking into a mudhole so deep, no vine or stick could possibly pull me out.

I'm staring at the gray floorboards of our porch when I feel the weight of Papaw's arm across my shoulders. "You did well, son," he says, giving me a big hug and then drawing Jules into it, too—bringing us gently together in the room of his arms. "The two of you made all of us here in Wonder Gap real proud."

"Yeah, Curley," Jules says. "We make a good team."

And then she kisses me on the cheek.

"I guess that makes us even." I smile, staring at her dimple.

"For now," she says.

———

Wonder—*noun*

1 : that emotion which is excited by novelty, or the presentation to the sight or mind of something new, unusual, strange, great, extraordinary, or not well understood; surprise; astonishment; admiration; amazement

2 : a cause of wonder; that which excites surprise; a strange thing; a prodigy; a miracle

Wonder—*verb*

1 : to be affected with surprise or admiration; to be struck with astonishment; to be amazed; to marvel

2 : to feel doubt and curiosity; to wait with uncertain expectation

W (continued...)

Papaw declares a *hiatus* (*h* word, last summer) on our words for the next few weeks. He says we need to catch up to our alphabet, and I need to catch up with school. He's right, of course. Now that Tiverton Coal has pulled out of Wonder Gap, hopefully for good, and the press ran our story, I only have three weeks of school left to study for final exams and to bring up my grades.

"Besides," Papaw said with that twinkle in his eye, "it's May in Wonder Gap and it makes sense to leave *wonder* running for a while."

There's plenty to wonder at, that's for sure. For one thing, we're finally getting warmer weather. The wild rhodies are out, dotting the woods in lavenders, reds, and flaming pinks. And Ma's white peony bushes on either side of the porch are throwing off a powerful scent.

Jules and I have been hanging out on top of Ol' Charley,

soaking up the sun as much as possible and studying. We quiz each other on history dates, biology terms, and such, so it's not as if we're sharing intimate secrets or anything. That is, until one pops out. It's about a week after our press conference, and we're studying for Mr. A's biology exam.

Somewhere between *osmosis* and *diffusion*, Jules blurts out of the blue, "JD and I broke up." She must see the blank look on my face, because she asks, "Aren't you surprised?"

"Yeah, I guess so. Well, no . . . *Maybe?*" Here Jules is telling me the news I've longed to hear ever since JD came to town, and I don't know *what* I think. "You guys have been acting differently ever since that day in the cafeteria when you stalked off in a huff. What happened?"

"Actually, we broke up that afternoon. He caught up with me after study hall and told me he was sorry about Ol' Charley, how he had been insensitive and all. You know me, I forgave him immediately." Yes, I do know her, which was why I told JD what she wanted to hear in the first place.

"Well, I wasn't sure what to say after that. I'd been thinking about breaking up with him for a while, but then, he was being so sweet about Ol' Charley, I just didn't have the heart." She drops her notebook off the trunk and pulls her knees up to her chin, facing me. "That's when he told me his dad is kicking him out of the house. He's moving back to Indiana to live with his mom right after school gets out."

Well, I about fall off Ol' Charley. I knew things were rough between JD and his dad, particularly since we posted our video on the Internet, but I had no idea it was this bad. Poor JD. He must feel like one of those transplanted elk that doesn't know where *home* is.

"Anyway, he thought it was best to break up now," Jules continues. "'No use postponing the inevitable,' he said." I overheard those exact same words the other night when Papaw and Aunt Gertie were talking about moving us up to Cincinnati.

Jules starts running the tasseled top of a long blade of grass up and down my bare arm, and I'd swear it's giving me goose pimples *inside* and out. "JD said I deserve somebody who understands me," she says, "somebody who shares my love for the mountains, that kind of thing."

All of a sudden, this change comes over her that's hard to describe. It's like she gets all soft and gauzy, and it's scaring me to death.

"When I asked him if he had anybody in mind, he just smiled and said he wasn't 'naming any names.' I think that's kind of weird, don't you?" And then she gives me this really pointed look. I mean, if it were any sharper, it would stick to my face.

So what do I do?

I shrug.

Yeah, that's right, I *shrug*, like I don't have a clue what she's talking about.

"Honestly, Curley. You're *impossible*," she says. And she packs up her book bag and stomps off in a huff. It's a familiar huff.

———

I know, I know. I missed my chance.

Believe me. I've been kicking myself for the last three weeks for not driving my truck straight through that barn door she was holding wide open for me. I mean, she had my name painted all over it.

In red.

With hearts.

I've tossed and turned and knotted up my bedsheets, fretting over what I should have said and what I should have done. Dang! I know I should have kissed her.

But how could I? I knew something I didn't have the heart to tell her yet.

I'd be leaving, too.

If you've ever looked up the *x* section in the dictionary, then you know there's not much to it, not even half a page. Papaw and I ran out of all the good *x* words several years ago, which is why he now gives me words in which the letter *x* plays an important part, as in *excellent* or *exasperate* (*x* word, last spring).

Papaw must know that leaving Jules and Wonder Gap is wringing my guts out, because the Sunday before school lets out, he gives me *excruciating*. It reminds me of the Cruciatus Curse in the Harry Potter books I devoured a few years ago—the curse that Voldemort inflicts on Harry that causes him such unbearable pain. I'm tempted to give Papaw the word right back, but I know he's just trying to be helpful.

"Sometimes, when you can put a word to something, it helps take the sting out," he said, but honestly, I think that's wishful thinking.

Jules knows by now, of course, that we're packing up to go. She stayed away for a whole week after I told her, but then her ma convinced her she was wasting valuable time that could be spent living.

We've taken to sitting on my front porch in the evenings having rocking chair races. I know that sounds crazy, but we like to pretend we're horses at the Kentucky Derby. The one who counts the most rocks from tip to tip "out of the gate" in sixty seconds wins. When we really get going, I'd swear you can hear the sound of hooves pounding the track. Anyway, it helps keep our minds off things. At least, that's what we're trying to do.

I don't know. If *excruciating* were a curse you were concocting like the one in the Harry Potter books, it would surely contain a pinch of play or a memory of joy. It seems that every second I spend with Jules these days makes the thought of leaving that much more painful.

It's even hard to say good-bye to JD.

Jules and I are racing rockers on my porch again when JD's ma drops him off for a few hours to hang out with us one more time before he leaves for Indiana the next day. I guess she came down for the weekend to pick him up.

We hand him the stopwatch and run a race to show him how we've been spending our time now that we're done with school and have saved our mountain—at least for now. We get him laughing so hard he about pees his pants, or so he says.

"You crazy hillbillies. It's a good thing I'm getting out of this God-forsaken place. If I stayed any longer, I might lose my cool."

I grab the stopwatch from his hand. "Too late, JD. You lost your cool as soon as you stepped foot in Wonder Gap, didn't he, Jules?" But Jules is sitting silently in her rocker with tears streaming down her cheeks.

"Ah, chill out, spunky girl." JD pulls her up and gives her a hug. "We said we weren't going to do this, right? Heck, we'll see each other more on the Internet than we ever did here in these hills."

"Not the same" is all she says, and we know she's right.

Later, we go in and watch a special news report I downloaded last Sunday about our campaign to save Red Hawk Mountain. They added a really nice interview with Helen sitting on Ol' Charley by my family's graves with Red Hawk rising in the background. Afterward, we check the counter on our You2CanChangetheWorld.com video for old times' sake.

Topless in Wonder Gap: 2,344,712 views and counting.

"Sweet," JD proclaims. "Not only are they featuring us up front now, but we're even attracting a few advertisers. Not bad for three scrawny, renegade teenagers from Wonder Gap, Kentucky. We *rock*, man!" We all exchange fist bumps, which is another thing I've learned how to do since JD came along.

"Yeah, man . . . we rock," I echo, but my words fall as flat as roadkill.

"Stick to your own way of talking, Curley, my man." JD slaps me on the back. "You've got way more cool than I'll ever have." High praise from the bad boy himself, and I'm basking in it when he adds, "Those Cincinnati chicks are gonna *love* you."

No sooner do those words come out of his mouth than we both know where and how they're going to land. Sure enough, Jules looks like a load of bricks just crashed right over her.

"Jules . . ." JD starts, but Jules gets up and gives him a hug.

"Don't worry, JD. You're fine. I need to get going, okay?" It's obvious that she's holding back tears.

"Sure," he says. "I'll call you this weekend . . . from Indiana, okay?"

"Sure," she says. "See you later, Curley."

Her hair curtains her face.

She slips out the back door.

All the joy in the room goes with her.

———————

Excruciating—*adjective*

: extremely painful, distressing, torturing, racking

By now, you might think that Papaw only gives me words that no kids my age have ever heard of. Sometimes, I think that, too. But then, after I get to know one of those words and use it? It climbs down from that hoity-toity tower I've put it on and lives with me where I walk.

Not all the words Papaw gives me are like that, though. Sometimes, he gives me a commonplace word that we use all the time—to wake me up to it, he says. I've learned those are the ones to watch out for. "Never take any word for granted," he tells me. "They all have the power to shape our world.

"I'm thinking of a word and it begins with *y*," Papaw says as he wraps one of his favorite mugs in newspaper and hands it to Aunt Gertie to pack in a box. We're leaving for Cincinnati in the morning.

I'm slumped over the kitchen table, taking a break from packing up my room. That's all I've been doing all day and I'm sick of it. "Papaw, can't we do this later?" I groan.

"Well, that most certainly is *not* the spirit of the word I have in mind." Papaw chuckles, as if anything could be funny right now.

I want to spit. I want to moan. I want to whine. Anything but work on this dang word he wants me to see. But, as you know by now, Papaw never gives up. The clues just keep on coming.

"I guarantee you, Curley, this word would make your life a whole lot easier, if only you'd choose to accept it."

Aunt Gertie looks over at me and then up into Papaw's face, real earnest-like. "Oh, John, why don't you let the boy be? Can't you see he's got a lot on his mind?"

Papaw gives her one of those warning looks that says, *Back off.*

That's what it's been like around here lately, and I have no reason to believe Cincinnati will be any different. It's obvious the two of them love each other, but Aunt Gertie has this way of stepping into places she doesn't belong. You'd think I'd like her taking my side, which is where she steps most of the time, but I'm used to fighting my own battles with Papaw and I'd like it to stay that way.

"That's okay, Aunt Gertie," I say, "I know what the word is, anyway."

"Is that a fact?" she says, flicking the end of a dish towel at Papaw's bottom.

"As a matter of fact . . . *yes*." I grin.

Papaw's beaming at me, like we've got our very own communication highway that nobody else can ride.

"Yes?" she asks, playing along.

"Yes!" Papaw and I shout as we exchange a high five.

And that's how I get this week's word, a short little number for an awfully big week.

Later, after Aunt Gertie has gone to bed, Papaw and I head for the living room, where I wrap myself up in one of Mama's crazy quilts, and Papaw builds a fire in the woodstove one last time, even though the night barely has a chill. I can't tell you how many "last times" I've counted over the course of the day, and now this. Our last night home.

"Why *yes*, Papaw?"

"I was hoping you'd ask." He pokes at the fire and it snaps to life. "Because *yes* is the most powerful word in the English language."

"But what about *no*, like what they're always telling us in health class?"

"Doesn't even come close."

"But, Papaw, we said no to Tiverton Coal, and that worked out pretty good."

"You're right, son. That *no* was powerful. But it was the *yes* that followed the *no* that really saved our mountain— the *yes* to Red Hawk, the *yes* to Ol' Charley, the *yes* to the life you and Jules love. Those two million viewers and counting were drawn like magnets to your resounding, heart-pounding *yes*."

So why don't I feel happy about it? Is there something wrong with me? Two million viewers, for crying out loud. Why do I feel so empty? I pull Ma's quilt up over my head, wishing the world away.

After a few minutes like that in the soft, sad dark, I feel the couch sink under the weight of Papaw by my side. I feel his broad hand press across my rounded back from shoulder wing to shoulder wing.

"Curley, my son," I hear his muffled voice say as he leans in close. "I know you don't want to leave, and I'm sorry."

Well, that does it. The floodgates break and my tears burst forth like a pent-up river, and no, I'm not too shy to admit it, and yes, I've got a powerful hurt. I throw the quilt off my head and wail, "I never said yes to leaving Wonder Gap, Papaw. I *never* said yes."

Papaw holds me as I cry. "I know, dear boy. I know. Just because you said no to losing your mountain doesn't mean you said yes to losing your way of life."

When my tears finally ease, he gets up and pokes the fire with a vengeance. It's as if he needs every burning ember to fuel his next words.

"Leaving all this?" He looks around. "I know it's not easy, Curley. Believe me, I know, it's tougher than dirt." At first I think he's gazing off into space, but then I realize he's staring at a picture of Ma and little Zeb on the mantel. He picks it up and studies it. "This needs to go with us," he says. He's been telling me all day we can bring anything we want. Aunt Gertie says we'll find room.

"Curley, I want you to know, I don't see us leaving Wonder Gap for good. I don't know how long it's going to take or how much it's going to take, but we're going to find a way to come back. I swear to God, Curley, I can feel it in my bones. These mountains aren't done with us yet."

"But how do you *know*, Papaw?"

"Well, I don't know, not really." He sits down in his favorite overstuffed chair across from me and peers into the picture he still holds in his hand as if he's searching for the answer.

"Curley, you know I'm not a churchgoing man, but I do believe in something. That something—call it God, call it Love, call it the Great Cosmic Glue for all I care—that *something* is always saying yes to our dreams, even when it looks like everything's falling apart. The secret to finding our way to those dreams is in saying yes back.

"When we lost your ma and little Zeb, there was no way I could have said yes to that loss. I just couldn't accept it. No way. But I did find the way to say yes to *you*. And you have made all the difference in my life." He sets the photo down gently on the table next to him.

"So you see, Curley, if you can't say yes to our leaving—and that's more than anyone should ask—then try to find a way to say yes to something else. I guarantee you it will ease your pain, and who knows? It might even give you something to smile about."

Papaw tries to smile at me as if to drive his point home, but it comes out looking pretty sad. Leaving can't be easy for him, either.

"Thanks, Papaw. You're the best," I say. We're always saying that to each other.

———————————

It's 1:00 in the morning, and the moon is two slivers shy of full. The path up to Ol' Charley is bathed in an eerie, blue-shadowed light. After Papaw went to bed, I snuck over to Jules's house and asked her to meet me. My heart is racing. I've come to say yes to her, but will she be there?

I search the open space around my family's grave site. Jules and I cut down the tall grass around Ol' Charley a few days ago, so I can see his outline clearly, his trunk lying long on the ground. My family's headstones are glowing like a row of dimly lit mirrors. I peer and peer at each and every shape in the night, but not one of them is Jules.

I settle into my favorite spot on Ol' Charley, near the wound where our special branch used to be. The moist mountain air settles on my skin. I pull the collar of my jacket up and clap my hands to warm them. Critters scatter in the brush.

"There you are!" I hear her voice before I see her. She emerges from the woods, breathless from her climb.

"*Jules,*" I say as she plops down beside me. Something says yes in me and I open my arms.

There's something about a *yes* that's been a long time in coming. It falls all over itself to get where it wants to go. That's what's happening now, up here at the Church of Ol' Charley. Instead of one kiss, like I've always pictured it, there are many. And not just on the lips, but all over her face.

At some point, I stop to make sure she's okay with all the kissing, but she just pulls me closer and nuzzles my neck.

"I brought you something," I whisper. "I found it when I was packing." I pull the dream catcher out of my jacket and finger its slackening web. "I don't know how you feel about it anymore, since I stole it from you and all, but I wondered if you might consider taking it back."

Jules puts her hand over mine and nods. We hold the dream catcher between us.

"Curley, I've been thinking," she says as she touches the hoop's tiny black feathers. "You know that journal I gave you for your birthday?"

"Yeah, you mean that homework that never ends? That was the best gift ever, Jules," I tease, even though it really was. She ignores me, as usual.

"Well, in addition to keeping your dictionary while you're up in Cincinnati, I was wondering if you'd write me your word every week . . . you know, so I can keep up with you. And then, I'll use your words to write you back."

"Gosh, Jules, a one-word letter? I guess I could do that."

She hits me on the arm, as if nothing's changed between us. "You know what I mean."

I do know what she means, and it sounds like more homework, but I decide to keep that to myself. Besides, she's letting me trace the contours of her face in the moonlight . . . and she's just about to smile.

Yes—*adverb*

: a word which expresses affirmation or consent

Synonyms: okay, all right, truly, indeed, no doubt, you bet, so be it, amen

A Note on Pronunciation

Papaw (Pá-paw)

Tsiwodi (Jee-woh-dee)
Cherokee for: "hawk."

Hoyana osda Unetlana wado (Hoh-yah-nah oh-s-dah Oo-nay-tlah-nah wah-doh)
Cherokee for: "We honor our good Creator, thank you."

Aho (Ah-hoh)
This word originates with the Lakota, but has been adopted by many American Indians, meaning "I agree."

Acknowledgments

In that the publication of this novel is a dream come true, my gratitude is as big as a mountain. First and foremost, I'd like to thank my agent, Brenda Bowen, for her wisdom and guidance, and for finding *Saving Wonder* the very best home. And to my gracious editor at Scholastic, Lisa Ann Sandell: Thank you for your discernment, your honoring ways, and for adding wonder, not only to the title, but to my first publication experience as well. A big thank-you also to Jim Tierney for the jacket art and chapter headings—and to all the people at Scholastic for their brilliant contributions.

I feel deep appreciation for all of my writing teachers, mentors, and colleagues throughout the years—particularly Judy Dekraker, Paul Bennett, Richard Kraus, Dom Consolo, Ethel Seese, Lisa Dale Norton, my friends from SCBWI Midsouth, and my Whidbey Island writing buddies, Theo Wells and Garr Kuhl. This novel was greatly enhanced by the insights of readers Tay Berryhill, Erin Barnhill, and Margo

Buchanan, as well as by Carnegie Center for Literacy and Learning instructor Marcia Thornton Jones.

I began this novel as a graduate student in Spalding University's MFA in Writing program and would not be the writer I am today without the brilliant mentorship and instruction of Joyce McDonald, Lesléa Newman, Rachel Harper, Julie Brickman, John Pipkin, David-Matthew Barnes, Ellie Bryant, Luke Wallin, and Susan Bartoletti, among so many others, including all of my Spalding peers. My heartfelt thanks go to Sena Jeter Naslund and Karen Mann for designing such an inspiring program, and to the MFA staff who make it all happen—Kathleen, Katy, Ellyn, and Gayle.

Research is the soil out of which a story grows, and to this end, I owe a huge debt of gratitude to my researcher, Carol Bischoff, and her contacts in the mining and archeological fields. I also appreciate Kaz of Kaz Woodcraft for teaching me about woodworking, and Scott Teodorski, a park ranger from Cumberland Gap National Historical Park, for his knowledge of the region. A very special thank-you to Kenneth Barnett Tankersley, PhD, for sharing his vast expertise in geology, archeology, and the Cherokee culture. You and the rest of my friends in the Cherokee and American Indian communities have helped me tell a better story.

My heart is full of gratitude for my Kali sisters, my e-circle sisters, and my soul friends—Kate, Nancy, Patricia, Terri, Cilla, Tamra, Liz, Anna, Christie, Linda, Susan A., Susan D., and Soni—as well as all of my friends in the Ahava community, who love and support me no matter what. Love and gratitude for my son, Zach, who is an unending source of inspiration, and for the rest of my beautiful family—Jennifer, Milo, Cassandra, Lou, Trey, Jason and family, Tiffany (I know you're there), Michael, and Rose—who have nurtured my dream in so many ways.

Finally, to my husband, live-in coach, and best friend for life, Richard: Thank you for being my *yes*.

About the Author

Mary Knight has lived in many awe-inspiring places—Traverse City, Michigan, and Whidbey Island in Washington State among them. She and her husband now reside in Lexington, Kentucky, where she loves the rolling green hills of horse country, exploring the Appalachian Mountains to the east, and watching University of Kentucky basketball. Most of all, she cherishes time with friends and family, who add great wonder to her life. *Saving Wonder* is her debut novel.